FI NOTES

FEMINIST WRITING ON ILLNESS & WORK

Edited by
Kirstie Millar, Laura Mehers,
Katrina Millar & Rosalind
Reynolds-Grey

Ache

Fit Notes:
Feminist Writing
on Illness & Work

Published by Ache, 2025.

ISBN: 978-1-0682858-0-6

Edited by Kirstie Millar,
Laura Mehers, Rosalind Reynolds-Grey
& Katrina Millar.

Copyright ©Ache 2025.
All rights reserved.

Cover Artwork: Cecilia Reeve.
Design: Theo Inglis.

Typefaces:
Zangezi by Daria Petrova,
Adobe Caslon by Carol Twombly,

Printed in the UK by Imprint Digital.

No part of this publication may be reproduced,
stored in a retrieval system, or transmitted,
in any form or by any means, electronic,
mechanical, photocopying, recording or
otherwise, without the prior permission of
the publishers. A CIP record for this book
is available from the British Library.

www.achemagazine.co.uk
Instagram: @helloachemagazine

Contents

—

NON-FICTION

—

Introduction

ACHE EDITORS

What does it mean to be chronically ill or disabled today? Politicians will bemoan your lack of work ethic, gesture at downward pointing charts and unfathomable figures, and blame you. 'This is your fault', they will say. This is your fault for not trying hard enough. For being trapped in a body that disobeys.

If you are working, you will anxiously monitor your body for signs of flare ups and pain spells. You will have sleepless nights worrying about money, or your dwindling paid sick days. When you sleep you will dream that your manager is angry with you (your manager will be angry with you). You will miss more than seven days of work and HR will demand a 'fit note'. If you are lucky your GP will offer you an appointment and provide you with the required letter (you might have to pay for it). A back to work meeting might be scheduled. Your employer might ask how they can better support you. Or your absence may have hit a 'trigger point' and your employer may require a formal 'intervention'.

If you are not working the guilt will feel heavy, it will tug at your chest. On some days you will mourn your lost usefulness, you will miss the busyness of your past life. But on other days, you will feel free. You will walk in the park in the middle of the afternoon, you will go swimming or sit in the warm grass and read a book.

You will always worry about money. You will apply for Personal Independence Payments (PIP). You will provide the required paperwork. You will be assessed ('Can you brush your teeth? How many meters can you walk without stopping? Can you prepare a meal for yourself?') Your application will be denied. You could appeal, but you will feel weary. You might feel ashamed, you might wonder if you are lying, if you are exaggerating your illness. (You are not, the system is designed to make you feel this way.)

In March 2025, Keir Starmer's Labour government announced an overhaul of the UK's welfare system. Starmer said that the cost of sickness benefits was 'devastating' for the country's finances, and that the current welfare system is 'actively incentivising' people to not work. This, Starmer argued, is 'unfair' to taxpayers and an 'affront to the values of our country.'

Fit Notes came out of the hostile, hateful language used by our government. We felt the need to join the ongoing discussion and invite chronically ill and disabled writers to explore their own complicated relationships with illness, work and labour. In this anthology an academic interrogates what it means to produce 'valuable work'. A poet joins the dots between rest, love and survival. A waitress wonders if Shakespeare's players ever skived from their acting jobs. A librarian removes forty-thousand books from a library and tends to her weeping fistula.

Sickness is an unavoidable part of life, whether we live with chronic health conditions or are knocked by brief bouts of illness. In a society that prioritises our ability to take up and maintain paid work, it is inescapable that our bodies and our illnesses are also intrinsically tied to our productivity. We are measured by our capacity for work, an inability to engage in work-related activities renders us ineffectual as individuals while acts of labour outside of this traditional sense of work – the labour of care, domesticity, love, parenthood, craft – are devalued and discarded.

In *Fit Notes*, our writers consider what it means to live now, under late-stage capitalism, in a society that prioritises productivity above all else, while living in a body that resists shift work and desk jobs and commutes. This anthology brings together nineteen writers who each interrogate illness, pain, gender and work. The writing is surprising, illuminating and potent. Our writers push back on the government's harmful rhetoric and reject claims of 'sick note culture' and 'lost productivity'. Our writers articulate what it means to live and work in a body that hurts.

For our cover art, Ache commissioned artist and animator Cecilia Reeve, who explored exhaustion, pain, stillness and time passing. Reeve's dreamlike painting shows us a private moment – a body at rest, with legs outstretched in a bathtub, skin soaking in luminescent, blue-green bath water.

Thank you for supporting *Fit Notes*, we hope the essays, poetry and fiction in this book resonate with you.

PART 1

✠

FICTION

Sick Note Culture

HATTIE ATKINS

1.

My first job was as a waitress, but I spent most of my time in the staff toilets, seeing stars and painting the porcelain with blood that shouldn't have been there, not for another two weeks anyway. I would listen to radio performances of Shakespeare plays to distract myself. I wondered whether Shakespeare's players skived from work, too, when their bodies bled and they couldn't feel their feet and they saw glitter and halos and Gods out of the corner of their eyes. Then I remembered that women weren't allowed to act in Shakespeare's day. Perhaps men acted out their clots and lesions, too.

You've asked me to talk through my CV. Another answer to your question – perhaps the one you'd prefer to hear – starts like this: my first job was in a tearoom serving cake and cocktails, before the tearoom expanded and we served brunches and dinners to keep up with the demand of a high street that didn't want us anyway.

I could give you this official *precis*, but it wouldn't tell the full story. It wouldn't explain how it ended, with the head chef standing outside the cubicle door, listening to me retch. He didn't say anything, but I knew it was him; I recognised his shoes. The next day, he told my colleagues he'd like to tear through me, if he could, and they laughed when they repeated it, and I went to the GP with my uterus beating like a heart in my hand.

[Aside] If you ask me for my working history, I'll play every role. I'll method-act. I'll live and breathe the characters. I'll stand outside the cubicle and I'll kneel on the floor by the cistern and I'll lean behind the bar upstairs, laughing along. I'll hear the story but I'll refuse to accept the sick note. I'll tell the girl in front of me that I don't believe in *over-medicalising the everyday challenges of life*, and that I expect to see her first thing in the morning.

2.

I was at university in London when I took my second job. I stalked the financial district, delivering leaflets for a high-end bakery eight hours a day, knowing that if I didn't finish the shift, I wouldn't get paid. There is no official version that competes against my version in this part of the story; this is how the job was sold to me, and this is how I'll tell it.

From house to house, from office to office, I walked under a sun like a hole, attempting to swallow me up. I held in place the heat pad that wouldn't stick to my stomach, my sweat having liquified the adhesive. My legs were tired my womb was tired my head was tired and my feet sliced open with every step. In my head, I rehearsed my lines for a university production of *King Lear*. 'When we are born, we cry that we are come to this great stage of fools,' I said.

[You've asked me for my working history, and I will relive it like a bad dream. You could, too; we could retrace my steps together, and I could prove I was economically active as well as physically, and you could feel the sweat and the sharp and the sting with me.

Or would seeing what I could once do turn you against me? Would you only see the kind of worker I could have been had I continued putting the hours in?]

[*OK, let's rehearse Act 2 again. This time, I'll limp. This time, I'll grind my teeth into dust and spit frogs from my mouth and shrivel down to the size of a plum stone. This time, we'll cover the route sixty times over. How long until your next appointment? Perhaps you should cancel it.*]

3.

I caught the flu at the start of my third job. For a fortnight, I lived in and out of a fever dream, stacking shelves as if I were still working my shift at the supermarket whilst the words spoken around my sickbed seeped into the open wound of my subconscious. It was the words of Shakespeare, mostly, whose plays I still listened to after dropping out of university. He told me that, when I yawn, 'hell itself breathes out Contagion to this world' whilst I put curds on the top shelf, jams on the bottom shelf, and I'd wake up with my head on fire and my skin on backwards.

I was summoned to a disciplinary. On the morning of the meeting, my bus was late, and I shivered at the shelter because I'd forgotten to put on tights. Or, rather, the polyester was liable to make my skin burn like hundreds of hot needles or a tick infestation, and today was just one of those days, I suppose.

In the disciplinary, they gathered behind the table like the witches in *Macbeth* and handed me their prophecy: They'd worry about my health if they were me. They'd certainly worry about me if they were my mother. They would try taking vitamins. They would try swimming to stay fit.

[*Aside*] Perhaps you'd say the same. Perhaps you're also 'solutions-focused'. You can't empathise with me because you too would encourage me to discuss *what work I can do, not what work I can't do.*

[*Aside*] Well, I can fold myself in two like a book. I can set myself on fire from the inside-out. I can make my uterus quiver like a frog slowly boiling in a pot of hot water. I can do all of this now if you think it would help. You need *greater medical evidence to substantiate my claim*, after all. What else would you like to see? What can I do for you? Can I get you anything else?

4.

When I take to the stage for my grand soliloquy, I imagine an audience, rapt and wide-eyed, but it is only you and you look bored, picking at something on the back of your head. No matter; I'd perform to a brick wall if I had to. It's the role I've been preparing for my whole life. I will turn my skin around so you can see all of me, every rotten bit, because today I am Juliet, bidding Romeo farewell. I am Hamlet on the verge of existential becoming. Now it's my turn to play each witch in *Macbeth*, boiling a toad 'i' the charmed pot'.

You ask if I'm able to concentrate on tasks at work. You ask if I'm able to travel to work, be on my feet for long stretches of time, wash myself, touch my toes, hold conversations, find God, relive the past, tell fact from fiction, advocate for myself. I hold the toad of my abdomen in my hands and step into the spotlight.

5.

It has never been *the flickering screen* for me. I have never been swallowed by the TV, the hole that people like me have been left to *sit before, alone* and *in the dark*. It has always been the stage. And so it swallows me now. You make marks on your paper like ticks or crosses or A*s or skulls and cross bones. I try not to watch your face for signs of approval, but when you appear unmoved, I fall deeper into the hole of my act. My symptoms can't prove themselves, or so you say, so I must prove them myself. Illness is a performance and all my body's a stage.

*

The assessment finishes, and you thank me for my time. I'll hear from you in ten working days. In the meantime, I'm to go back to work.

I'm led back through the office with a chaperone, then left at the door. I cross the car park alone.

In the car, I tell my mum how it went and when I'm likely to hear back.

She looks at me like she used to after one of my auditions and says, "well, fingers crossed you get it."

—

Quotations in italics taken from 'Prime Minister's speech on welfare: 19 April 2024' *https://www.gov.uk/government/speeches/prime-ministers-s peech-on-welfare-19-april-2024.*

Other quotations taken from the following William Shakespeare plays in order of appearance: *King Lear* (1608), *Hamlet* (1603) and *Macbeth* (1623).

Refurb

LAURA ELLIOTT

Two weeks into the job they ask me to empty the library. Three floors of books and no plan, they say, you have one month.

It is summer, I am wearing a thin monochrome checked shirt-dress and I feel strong, for once. Something about the air on my skin as I scoot through the park in the dappled mornings.

I've been having dreams where he comes into the kitchen, looks me up and down, slips his fingers underneath my skirt to feel the crinkled fabric. Touches my thighs accidentally.

There are maybe forty-thousand books in the library. The roof has caved in so we cannot enter the upper floors, and the tap water is not safe to drink.

The security guards bring us bottles from the corner shop but so much single-use plastic makes me sick. I refill a few at home and carry them back in my bag every morning, with my spare underwear and just-in-case dressings.

I am strong enough for this. A high point where I can just tamp some gauze between my bum cheeks to absorb the drainage. I wrap the soaked pads in tissue and post them into the sanitary waste bin and think, this is not that bad.

I devise a plan with multiple evacuation stages. During stage one, staff from other sites come and choose which books they want to take away. I have to trust them all. They obliterate the kinder boxes and travel guide section but leave the cookbooks untouched.

We are in the middle of a heat wave. The library is an ex-telephone exchange with sheet glass windows that do not fully open. The safari mural painted on the wall is sponsored by a software company that no longer exists.

I begin to weed the teenage non-fiction and find a book by a celebrity judge about being cool at school. Should you speak to the new kid on the bus? You don't owe him a thing!

At lunchtime I sit alone in the makeshift staffroom, which is actually the children's library, to eat salty cheese and olive pastries and mild ajvar straight from the jar with a spoon.

I am wearing loose linen shorts and an oversized pink shirt with jazzy scribbles on it. I close my eyes and let the sun press my body deep into the black leather armchair until we are one fused skin.

Everybody else comes back with fast food, the bin overflows with burger slips and chicken buckets. Abruptly I realise nobody has been emptying the rubbish, the bathroom smells like all the worst parts of me. I move into the cooler offices downstairs and don't say anything.

During stage two, we skim off all the books we don't want. We tip them face down on the shelves, or pile them around the edges of the library to distinguish them. The first floor window sills thicken with violet and fuchsia stacks of worn out romances and family sagas.

My fistula has started to throb, it feels like a bulb has formed somewhere inside. In the shower I press it and it is hard and sore. Something dark dribbles out. Probably nothing, I think and masturbate anyway, imagine the murky stalactites that descend in the archive stacks are forcing me down, coiling into me.

All my most recent sexual fantasies involve me being tricked into it somehow. He is leaning over to check the time, his breath on the back of my neck and oops, his hand is inside my trousers and he's not asking whether it hurts.

There is always some kind of slime in my pants, one way or another.

I am gradually revealing facts about myself to my new colleagues. For example, they know I have a daughter. I want them to understand this is not the most interesting thing about me but all our conversations get stuck on her.

She is nearly two years old, I say, realising only as I repeat myself that I have been sick now for so long and it is more or less the same.

Stage three is supposed to remove the dead stock but the drivers fail to arrive. Each morning I call the company in frustration, only to be reassured, tomorrow they will come, they will take twenty crates, thirty maybe.

I take a photograph of security drowning amidst stacks of retired footballers' biographies, of the late summer light half blocked out by crime fiction duplicates on the window ledges. I try and fail to book a doctor's appointment, again.

Nobody has blocked off the returns box from the outside and books thump into the metal bins periodically, mocking our lack of progress. The sanitary bins are so full up the lids won't close. The smell permeates the upper floors, or it is on me, my fingertips, I can't be certain it's not.

What are we going to do about the fourth floor, someone asks, and I laugh because I think they are joking.

Through the windowless staff offices where the servers perpetually hum, behind some abandoned office chairs and a torn to pieces antique leather throne, is the reference library. The books are either completely worthless or incredibly valuable and I have no time to research any of them.

The manager of the removal company finds me on my knees pretending to count the atlases. They are going to strip out the double-sided shelving, then what. Everyone is so efficient and here I am trying not to faint when I sit down.

He starts to tell me about living in the countryside, how long it takes him to lock up in the evening because of all the animals he has to feed. There is a hedgehog, he says, and a stoat.

I have a friend who once stopped traffic for a rogue white ferret, I reply. All the locals knew who it belonged to.

Afterwards, on social media, the owner posted a thank you to 'the lass who helped catch my ferret'. He was a drug dealer and the ferret was called Ghost.

I become acutely aware of how close together we are standing, and that the gauze in my underwear is soaked through. I can feel the wetness clinging to the skin, fibrous as fruit pulp. I wait for him to leave before reaching behind me to check if it has seeped through the seat of my jeans.

I can feel the abscess now when I walk. It fits in the palm of my hand and is hot, like a soft boiled egg. The discharge is thicker, and it bleeds, I don't know what this means.

The next morning I am at the hospital by 8am. I pass through the metal detectors to urgent care triage, where the anticipated waiting time on the digital board is twelve and a half hours.

I am wearing a black, long-sleeve t-shirt with a picture of an orange snake tunneling through the eye socket of a green skull surrounded by a lightning storm. Nobody comments on it.

A tall man with no trousers is apologising to everyone around him, he is in too much pain to get dressed properly. He wears his deck shoes like sandals, crushing the heels, and a brown peacoat that only just reaches the tops of his thighs. Despite this, or perhaps because of this, he is the most charming person in the room.

I wait for two hours, nearly three. I have brought the wrong book. It is about a woman who wants to murder her sister. I am not sure I care enough.

I try not to worry about the library but continue to refresh my email browser, increasingly agitated by the same error screen. I let four different people insert their fingers in me. Yes, it hurts, it hurts more, should it hurt?

I am given some antibiotics and told it's probably nothing. I am so bored of waiting I will believe anything that means I can leave, even though I had resolved before coming not to let them win.

On my way out, the man with no trousers is trying to sit down. Everybody around him is engaged in the act, holding onto some part of his body, lowering him into the chair as he groans politely. One woman has both her hands on the back of his bare, hairy thighs.

When I arrive at the library, the staff are frenzied, I am smoke entering a beehive. In my absence, they have built and packed two hundred cardboard boxes full of withdrawn books. The new book disposal company I secured in a daze has delivered six wooden pallets and an industrial cling film to wrap it all up in.

I am delighted and my colleagues laugh around me. We build up another pallet and I send everyone home early, wrap it myself slowly, ceremonially. I resist the urge to kiss the shiny new skin, to lay down on top of it and tuck myself inside the plastic.

The best aftercare for a fistulotomy is to pack the open wound, daily, with a kind of jellied ribbon, and cover it with an absorbent adhesive dressing. This way it heals from the inside out and you avoid the hollow sealing over, reinfecting.

I would rather have a new wound each day than have an old wound reopened, observed a friend.

The first time I realised I was sick, I was on holiday. There was the long hot weekend in the eco-cabin among the spiked apple trees and the pouring rain holiday by the sea, and in between stretched a whole summer of maternity leave, of relentless cluster feeding just to get the baby to sleep.

I made it all the way to the south coast on the train before collapsing. Even then I was determined to make the most of it. We walked four miles along the beach path from the tidal island to the town centre, the wind blowing so hard off the sea it scorched my left cheek.

We shared mugs of orange wine and cheese pasties in the evening, rolled dice on the carpet and watched the top twenty most expensive music videos ever made, the volume turned so low on the television it may as well have been muted.

At night I sweat through the sheets and blamed the stuffy cottage curtains, the baby co-sleeping between us. A local artist's canvas hung above the bed's head and I had nightmares of the whorls puckering, clenched and unfurling like a thousand awful orifices.

I woke up each day in excruciating pain and spent all morning blunting it back down again with pills. I spent hours on hold trying to speak to anyone, anywhere, who would help me.

Why isn't it working, I demanded, squatting in the kitchen, rattling through the blister packets as the baby screamed.

Take her out and buy some more, maybe the branded ones are more effective, I say, even though I read an article that clearly explains why they are not.

There are five days left to empty the library. The building has been so tired for so long.

I am invited to a symposium on collection management software in the basement of a hotel in the centre of the city. The room is too small and the organisers keep apologising for the last minute venue change but really they are asking the men to stop touching us on purpose.

I am grateful for the excuse to leave the library. The vibe is weird and fraught and there are more and more questions I cannot answer.

I find a seat near a familiar colleague and drink too much awful coffee just to have something to do. I am wearing loose brown corduroy trousers and a sheer striped velvet turtleneck. We discuss benchmarking and I complain about the consortium book recycling company and my hands shake because I perceive myself to be, as always, far too earnest.

I anticipate a break in the programme and run to the bathroom, relieved to skip the queue. It is only when I am bent double, trying to focus the reflection of my arsehole in the chrome flush button, that I catch sight of myself, atomised, in the mirrored mosaic tiles and realise the extent to which I have habitualised this sickness.

This is not normal, I reprimand myself, as I lay tissue on the toilet seat to catch the rusty drips. The cubicle is tight and I can hear the women begin to assemble beside the washbasins, nylon coats rustling, whilst I milk the pus from my abscess, again.

There is no way the next person won't smell all of this, but I just need to release a little pressure, just to get me home safe.

Remind me again, says the colorectal surgeon, fingers deep inside me. You have an inflammatory bowel disease? You had an injury? Remind me, he repeats, you have a child? It was a difficult labour? Maybe you're just unlucky?

I stand at the centre of an empty library. Track marks where the shelving sat so long it scarred the carpet, a few out-of-date cancer pamphlets scattered about the place.

The majority of the children's books were so sun damaged they weren't worth keeping, the pages yellowed and flaking apart like dried fish.

I realise I never actually measured anything, the full métrage of the shelving, the distance from one bracket to another, how many face-on displays there were. It's okay, I reason, I have been good enough.

I fill a postal crate with ice and dunk three bottles of champagne. Somebody has bought some cheese straws and sweet chilli rice crackers. The new library will have a performance space and a rooftop bar, I've been told.

We will lose an entire floor to the business centre and there will be many, many more surgeries.

That is a problem for twenty-twenty-six I begin a new habit of saying, clacking my plastic cup against my colleagues' and locking eyes with each of them in turn, just in case.

You must have a very high pain threshold, said the examining nurse, finally.

I refuse to look at the wound but I can describe what it looks like precisely. Face down on the floor the evening after the third surgery, I guide him in removing the sodden bandages. It is not supposed to be this wet, I am familiar now.

I have spread the clear plastic mat beneath me that we normally use to protect the carpet from highchair dinner spills. I am wearing a black hoodie and tracksuit bottoms and I'm still baggy from general anaesthetic.

There is not looking at it or looking accidentally or having to look. There is dealing with the thing in front of you, which is the wound. When everything is the wound and the wound is a void and the library is finally empty.

It looks just like a ruby, he says.

Pigeon-Toed

CAT CASEY

The Bartender held no illusions about it; she did not possess attractive feet. The second toe of each foot was long, the rest of them clubbed and oddly shaped. Her skin stretched tight and thin across the tops to create hill ranges from her prominent metatarsals, and her heels often cracked until they bled.

Knowing that her feet were ugly, it shocked her immensely when she was propositioned at work earlier that week. It was a regular, B3, who always drank Woodford Old Fashioneds and was memorable for the fact that he was remarkably ugly. He was nearly bald save the ring of thin, limp hair that came down to his shoulders, with a face that resembled a bowl of cottage cheese. His eyes were very large and pale, and tended to water in the fluorescents of the bar lights. The Bartender often felt unnerved to look up from her phone or a half-mixed cocktail to see those eyes staring directly at her from his spot at the bar.

'Let me rub them,' he had said. 'Please.'

The Bartender laughed in the way she did when she was uncomfortable but still needed to pay her rent, and pretended that he had been joking. B3, evidently the Foot Fetishist, did not let up.

'Please,' he said again, 'I'll pay you.'

This was harder to ignore, but then the door opened, and the Bartender moved to greet a young couple who thought it appropriate to bring their baby to a bar just because it served food, so she was saved from answering.

Unfortunately, the Bartender had been wearing the wrong shoes for weeks: thick chunks of platform on concrete flat floors which made her entire lower half feel like she was a snap pea waiting to be cracked. At night, she'd lie in bed with atrophied legs, afraid to lift the covers to see shriveled up, deflated balloons where her limbs used to be. On her days off, she could hardly do anything but sit and lie down, having spent so much of her work week standing.

Friday had been the worst. Three kegs had kicked within her first hour on the clock, and she had to lug the giant casks of beer up and down the stairs from the back walk-in to change them. Her body ached.

According to the Manager, the Bartender is only allowed to sit down when there are no customers present at her bar. On this particular day, they all seemed to know this; each of them arriving just as the last one left, keeping her from taking the weight off her legs for the sake of a two-dollar tip.

She wanted nothing more than to go home, crawl into her bed covered in unfolded laundry, and call out of her next shift. But she was short on rent and had gotten the third very scary, red-ink letter from her credit card company in the mail that morning. So, when the Foot Fetishist appeared again, sitting on the edge of her bar in his normal stool, and looked at her with those milk-glazed eyes, she simply sighed deeply and nodded her head.

The Foot Fetishist lived in a house much nicer than the Bartender, who was fearing perhaps an old slaughterhouse or a sex dungeon, had expected. The wallpaper was old and crumbling in places, and the appliances needed updating, but it was otherwise inoffensive. Sitting primly on the edge of a worn-in sofa, she swallowed a laugh. How absurd to mind her manners in her current situation.

'So,' she said. 'What do I do?'

'Nothing,' the Foot Fetishist replied quickly, like all the letters were fighting to be the first one out of his mouth. He was breathing very loudly. 'Just sit there.'

The Bartender shrugged as if to say 'have at it', and let her back fall against the cushions. She could feel his breath on her exposed ankles, and slowly, waited to feel it on her feet too. Despite herself, she found that she was almost excited. At the very least, anticipatory. It'll be nice for someone to take care of her, she thought. It'll be nice to have someone want to care for her, even if it was so very strange.

Maybe this could be a regular thing. She didn't mind the extra two hundred dollars in her back pocket, and even though the Foot Fetishist repulsed her, it had been a very long time since she had felt any hands on her skin besides her own. It was nice to absorb warmth off someone else. She had forgotten that.

His hands carefully came up to cup the heel of her left foot and the Bartender was surprised when she blinked, and her lashes came away wet. Here was someone; this poor, very sweet, very ugly man, who liked even her worst parts. The parts of her stolen away by years of standing, running between tables, cheap work shoes, twelve-hour shifts without a break or a meal or even a moment just to stop, sit and breathe. The parts she had traded in for a paycheck.

She opened her mouth to thank the Foot Fetishist, for something she didn't exactly know words for, when she felt his skin leave her abruptly.

'I'm sorry,' he said, fishbowl eyes not meeting hers, 'I can't do it. They're just too ugly.'

'What?' She said, suddenly too exposed with her bare feet on a stranger's carpet.

'They were supposed to be different. I always pictured them different,' he said, and the Bartender wished that made her feel better, to know that she did not fit whatever idea this stranger had of her – that there was no one out there who, at night, thought of the *real* her, the one with bad credit, clubbed toes and ingrown nails. As she gathered her shoes and her socks and left quickly with the money still in her jeans, she wanted the fact that she didn't even have to earn the cash to soothe the aching in her chest, but all she felt was the weight of the bills in her back pocket.

CAT CASEY

Venus of Stalling, Battersea

T. LAUNDY

My estimates, I don't manage. That's the particular loop I've been up in since my mum died, and I've tried not to kick off each time. I don't manage mostly. My memory's not great. So, she died two years – no, no. It's three years ago now, it is. She died in the February, one of those horrible February days where it's a grim, blue dark too early. I came back with the shopping for her, and I remember walking into the bedroom and I go, I've got your shop, and she doesn't seem to say much. But I do swear she made a noise, and I made us cups of tea. She didn't say much to me at that point really, she talked less and less with time, just grunted, watched telly, playing things on her tablet. She took decaf tea, I don't, just normal, and I set it down on her side table in the bedroom. The bedroom covered in the thick, blue dark light fringing the evening. I think, oh, I've got the teabags wrong. Put the teabags in the wrong cups, got decaf in mine. I laugh, I say, oh mum, wait I've gone and got teabags wrong, but she's not even turned over. Just got her back to me. And I'm talking away at her, but she wasn't, you know. I watch all sorts of films, especially now, and whenever I watch a film and, you know The Notebook? Like that, extremely high emotion where everything happens really quickly. People die all dramatically, and in the film people cry for them just like right there. And I did cry when I shut up and realised she wasn't going to say anything back, but I don't think it was because I was going to cry right there because she's dead, and I am sad she's dead, I think it was just... well, it seemed like what was supposed to happen. I sat on the bed with her petting her face and saying, oh mum. Oh mum, that's all I could say. That's all I said at the funeral too.

I do get worse around the February. It was the February year after she died that I started seeing women. My mum died of bits associated with her condition. She had a lot wrong with her, not one big thing mostly, just lots of bits, then she got COPD and she slowed down a lot and then she just couldn't do anything anymore, it all just got into her, her spirit, I think, that her body wasn't working. Because her mum, my nan, had bits wrong too, she had glaucoma and bits and pieces and she was only upright most of the time because my mum was propping her up. My mum cared for my nan for maybe sixteen years? She hated it. She said, don't let me get like that. But I did. But, she loved my nan. There were times when you wouldn't blame her if she said she didn't. She did what she could for nan even when she was difficult. When my mum did start needing care she, well, it was her turn to become difficult, I mean, she didn't set out to be, but I think it was a bit of a living nightmare for my mum. Becoming her own nightmare. Not that she hated nan, it's just, you know, it's complicated. Complicated being so responsible. And she'd swapped places and was on the other side. She was an amazing carer, she thought of everything anyone could've needed and it helps, obviously, when you're very close to someone and you know what they're like, but my mum actually worked as a carer for most of her life anyway so it all came naturally to her. Not like me, I was off trying to... I don't know, thinking of *the cinema* and just caught up in culture. Wanted to become a screenwriter, actually, but yeah, when it was my turn to look after my mum, bugger having a scooby. It was a real trial. I'd watched her with my nan and learnt the basics but people have specific needs, and god, if they're particular, they need everything to be in a proper specific way. And when someone doesn't get out as much, you need to like, cater to the moods of a person, they get miserable. That's why I'm like this too. I wasn't that good with that sort of thing. We would fall out a lot. I think my mum died before I got the chance to be the best carer for her.

I did drugs when I was younger, bit less as I got older, and I think something happened. I think something went a bit off in my brain. Uni was this blur of attempting to, I don't really know... visualise myself as this sort of auteur or whatever, who had these big ideas about films. But I grew up and realised what films were actually like, let's not even get into it, with this country, and the industry, and that's when I just didn't have any sort of plan. I smoked a lot of weed, I did this and that every few weeks, I don't want to go into it. It's the only way to try and explain it, really, what I get, because otherwise I don't have much else to go off. Don't know whether anyone else in the family ever had these problems.

I see 'funny women'.

So I don't have a job and that's the ache at night. I can't work because I can't deal with it. Trying to explain that is what you'd call a quagmire. It's not because I don't want to, it's because you got to be consistent. People want to know you all over in a way that makes sense, and when I'm in a job I don't make sense, I never make sense. Uni made me think I should do something useful because I could feel the cement of society swallowing me all the time. Mum wanted me to figure it out, so I went for nurseries. There's something I think everyone can do when they think of kids, which is trying to picture yourself as this person who can be… admired, and responsible, and safe. I don't know. If you can be this shelter for something so little and new and half-formed, then you can see yourself as being strong like they do. I do like that. But I weren't any good at it at all. I was just always in moods, and I wouldn't even want to be there, then I'd get this bad feeling about a colleague or one of the kids would act up or hit me and I'd avoid going in because – it's a feeling of dark empty. None of the other women really liked me, maybe because I wasn't good at making decisions or just taking initiative and everyone had to tell me what it was I had to do. I tried three different nurseries with stints of things inbetween. First time was because it was a direction, right, second was because I wanted to show I could really do it, and the third was because I didn't know what else I was supposed to do. Death sentence was when I got in safeguarding trouble, end of the third time. It was, three women turned up to pick up a littlun. They were like Russian dolls, they were in height order. I thought they did not look anything like the mum who usually comes to pick him up, but they said they were picking him up to take him somewhere, and I just believed them, I don't know… I got fired for being on CCTV taking him to the bus stop and leaving him there. Mum just died. Police were involved. Maybe the papers, but I don't remember very well because I was on all sorts. It was my only ward time before, and it was long enough, and I don't want to talk about it, I already talked about it. I don't want to think of these white mausoleums. I don't like children anymore. I mean, really, how could I? Motherhood was this dying thing in me already, like a dried out thing in a jar, and my mum was shrinking in the brine of life, she was so small, like a child. Ever smaller and paler. My mum was my mum and then I was her mum. Funny women are where mums become hidden underground. They're round, with odd little faces like... what's that word, impressions of thumbs in the features. They come and go... listening to you mope in the walls. Reading over the shoulder.

I'm kicking off again, sorry.

I've been under the old jobcentre. Frequented it when I was in my mid-20s and I got very ill between jobs, then I got moved to the other one near Stockwell a few years ago. I've been looking for a carer for a year now. I've got some sort of rot in my lower spine which has been fortifying itself. That sort of thing, you just have to look at where you're going to go with it. So I was a big girl and said, right, we're going to have a chat with Kandice, the one with the mouth. She's my social worker, we're going to talk to her about what we can get. Progress has been so slow. Kandice isn't very well, bless... We talked about my options before she went into hospital to have her baby, but she was already fit to burst. I've been in the lurch since. I called up, then, a few weeks ago to check on where we were with it, because that day I'd had to do this bit with a cab to get back from the shop, I'll spare the details as it's not particularly nice. But, we need progress. The bloke on the end was not very helpful but he said something about the jobcentre, the old one on – he goes, that must be really difficult for you, all that they go on with, we have this service at here, but it's all this, but he mentioned that jobcentre and I don't know, I just thought fine, I'll go there thank you.

Underneath it there's a hole. Tunnel. The jobcentre bloke stayed on the phone a while to get me through the building, which I thought was good, because he didn't have to do that, that sort of extra mile work. He was worried about me getting lost. I was glad for it before the reception died, he said it would, because I was thinking about how the place wasn't really accessible because I can't see where I'm going, but he said that it's a bit of a last resort and they don't like offering it much, luckily I'm not bedbound yet otherwise he absolutely wouldn't have said anything about it. Then off goes the reception and I'm on my own. Me and mum's walking stick with its frame clinking, grinding impact with the wet. I'm going to myself, there's seats when I get there.

I walked on a fair bit into the half-dim there. Then I'm at this place which is just this pit, there's ashes all over the floor, all covering the legs of the chairs, just your normal waiting room chairs with the maroon cushion bits like you get at outpatients, and the walls are crumbling with loose mud. Not very well lit either, I'd add. It's very quiet and there's not really any other people – I think, I didn't notice because there's a photo, right, a big, well, not too big, but it's bigger than any photo I've got of her. It's a photo of my mum in the centre, just on the floor. Part of me wanted to do something about it, but I didn't want to just jump up and grab it, because of course that's my mum, but – I end up sitting near this older Indian lady there and she's grumbling away at herself, then she starts saying to me about the lights, and she's right! I said, that's what I was thinking. Then I pointed at the photo and I go, that's my mum. And she pulled this face a bit like she was impressed, you know. Maybe she knew something I didn't. We're all there for a bit, and it starts to get a little dark. I see the funny women in the blacker bits of the room, with their big bellies. There for me. That all gets, like, into me, until my name gets called, and I'm at this desk with, no word of a lie, the most beautiful thing I've ever seen, no lie. Not sure if it was a man or a woman, don't take that the wrong way, but it glowed at me when it talked. Like light on the sea. I said, you've got a photo of my mum. And it replied, only a little voice and it said, oh, we share the waiting room, it gets lent out. Then it's down to business, and of course I end up crying a bit. The light of it bounced off mum's photo into my eyes so she's there shining at me the whole time. They ask, why do you need care? And it seems every single question is just a rewording of that. Asking me if I've already tried this and that, maybe I have, maybe I haven't. At one point it asks me if I have anyone who can be used as reference, for me as a patient, that's dodge isn't it? I put your details down, but I'm not sure whether you're happy about that, now I've told you about it all.

It said: I'll add you to our waitlist, but if I'm honest (but they're only so honest) it could be a while. It went on, they always go on, it said, we'll try and keep you updated in the next few weeks, we're just understaffed and a manager is on leave or something. But hopefully things will move along and I'll know as soon as possible. The leaflet I got wasn't half old fashioned, wait 'til you see. Then I went home. I'll call the number in a week, maybe, they all get so arsey if you haven't waited adequately.

A funny woman with extreme shapes mournfully delivered the letter that detailed my jobcentre appointment, the one for the back and forth about the change in my benefits after mum died, when I'd no longer be a registered carer. What sort of slips do they get in actual companies, or the council and all that, when you're a carer with them? I checked mum's documents before and didn't find much about it. Just a lot of post-its calculating bills and what I think, actually, is a statue of me.

T. LAUNDY

The Signs

VIDA ADAMCZEWSKI

SIGN ONE

OPEN

SIGN TWO

Written out this morning on a piece of pristine folded card, the sign on the desk looks out over the shop like pride rock. It replaces a flimsy paper notice that was taped wonkily to the till. The sign is written in green ink, reminiscent of primary school. Because green is non-threatening, non-accusatory, non-disciplinary. Green is optimistic, it sees the best in people. Green says 'could be better' but in green. The sign's predecessor was written in red. It said 'this bookseller has chronic fatigue FYI' and was read as too aggressive, except by those who thought it was an example of the bookseller's sardonic humour and asked her, glinty eyed, if it was a joke. Green is too earnest to be read as a joke. It is the colour not quite of pride, but of accommodation.

The sign says 'Please Be Patient. This Bookseller Has Chronic Fatigue. Thanks!' In ideal conditions, these three sentences prompt three thoughts in the customer's head. Firstly: of course, I always am. Secondly: Oh, I see. In that case, I certainly will be. Thirdly: You're welcome. The conditions in the customer's head are not always ideal.

This kind of overt public disclosure in the workplace to complete strangers – not even to your boss, or the head of HR, or your colleague – is the result of the specific demands of customer service on the ill body.

Before the sign, the bookseller would arrive at work pallid and tired and usually five or ten minutes late and would be asked by the first, eager, usually five or ten minutes early customer if she was hungover. She would weather the sighs or foot tapping of customers waiting – patiently – to purchase their tasteful cream books of autofiction (without exception cream books written by ill women who doubtless had their own signs. In fact, the cream books themselves were signs). Once she was told she was rude by a customer who loomed over her as she sifted through a still-boxed delivery for a book that had been ordered the day prior. She had emitted a sigh of her own as she squatted down by the box, another as she dragged a second box towards herself. She had perhaps too brusquely said I know the one when the customer began to describe the cover of the book in detail. The bookseller now has the sign as protection like a squat bodyguard. A talisman. And an excuse.

And therein lies one of the bestest pleasures the sign has given the bookseller: plausible deniability. Because the sign is also sleight of hand. Did that bookseller roll her eyes at me? Or was that merely the fluttering lids of a woozy invalid?

A surprising side effect of the sign is that the sign invites the customer's own disclosures. Not wishing to fall into the Black Books cliche of hostility, the bookseller listens attentively, and smiles while punching the numbers into the till. But she must admit she feels that listening to the customer's description of their symptoms and their labyrinthine struggles with the NHS is, regrettably, beyond her paygrade. The sign does not say 'This Bookseller Has Patience' and yet, in some way, it does.

More common than disclosure is sudden onset selective blindness. Embarrassed by the sign, as they are by the brace the bookseller sometimes wears, the customer's eyes merely glaze, drop, or hover over the bookseller's shoulder. Or perhaps they clock the sign, lock eyes with the bookseller and, as they might the blue badge that asks for their seat on the bus, set their jaw and pretend they have not seen the sign. Once, the bookseller repeated the words of the sign to the customer, when they were using this tactic. Once, the customer apologised.

The sign has also been known to pique curiosity in the customer. The customer looks at the bookseller like a vet looks at a hamster, or a man looks at a female artist's painting. Is this bookseller exhibiting symptoms, they ask. The bookseller does not always feel obliged to answer the customer's question, but often. After all, the bookseller invited their questions with the sign. The sign in this case is a kick me sign, self administered.

In all these cases, the sign has the effect of making the bookseller more visibly human to the customer. The cases diverge along lines of how welcome this humanity is. For the bookseller behind the sign, it is interesting working out whether she prefers her humanity to be on display.

The morning passes. The sign remains in state.

SIGN THREE

Back in five! Lunch!

SIGN FOUR

In the storeroom there is a sign. When the bookseller slips behind the hidden door to dismantle boxes or heat up her lunch in the microwave or replenish the birthday cards, she sees it. She has never read it in full but she has read snippets of it that over time must make up the whole. The sign details the respective health and safety obligations of her employer and herself, the employee. The sign features images of men in hardhats and a woman with a clipboard in a maroon v-neck. The health and safety obligations are non-descript. They are generalised. The obligations include the obligation to discuss and agree health and safety procedures specific to the workplace.

While the bookseller is waiting for her lunch to finish spinning round and round in the microwave, she thinks about the possible hazards that her job presents. She thinks the greatest hazard is probably the way she sits directly on the oil filled electric radiator in the winter until her jeans are hot and stiff to the touch. The second greatest hazard is the way she lifts the boxes of books onto the desk to sort through them. She has never been good at lifting with her legs. People say it to her, and she says it to other people when they complain about their sciatica, but still she can only wrap her arms around the boxes, tip herself forward and then lever herself back. The third greatest hazard is the small, snot sticky hands of children who tornado into the shop after school. The fourth greatest hazard is the microwave. Which pings now, and when she opens the door, the wheel keeps turning and the machine continues thrumming until she switches it off at the wall.

She takes her lunch to the desk. The fifth greatest hazard is her lunch, which is very hot soup and burns her tongue when she eats it. The sixth greatest hazard are the sharp shelves themselves, laden with too many books that sometimes fall down when caught by the draught from the door. The seventh greatest hazard is the door, which does not have a buffer and sometimes crashes quite violently behind the customer who leaves too quickly, without saying goodbye. The eighth greatest hazard is the carpet, which rears up unexpectedly beneath the bookseller and makes her trip when she is carrying her empty bowl back to the storeroom. The ninth greatest hazard is her bowl which is ceramic and could shatter on the floor of the storeroom. The tenth greatest hazard is the customer, who, having read the sign on the desk, asks how come she is at work, if she is ill. The bookseller says she has to pay her rent and besides she likes serving customers, selling books. This job is good for her, she says. The eleventh greatest hazard is the sign, which she looks at again when she closes the storeroom door behind her, the sign which does not forewarn her of the relevant hazards or how to manage them.

SIGN FIVE

Back shortly (time unspecified)

SIGN SIX

In the toilet the sign is next to the mirror. It offers advice to booksellers who are suffering from stress. It suggests buying a lavender plant, staying hydrated, taking deep breaths, and remembering that the customer's anger is not your fault. The bookseller rubs her eyes and looks at herself. Emotions are subjective experiences, the sign says. Her bowels just emptied themselves so violently that she thinks she might now look visibly thinner. She practises her smile. Once, twice. She fills up a glass of water and returns to the desk, removing sign five from the door and holding the door wide open for the customer and the customer's buggy.

The customer's children press the same button on the book over and over again, cutting the tin can version of Swan Lake off again and again at the fifth bar. It commences again each time with the orchestra warming up, then the long flat note of the instruments being tuned.

The customer appears at the desk. The bookseller watches the customer's eyes with interest as they flicker along the words on the sign. The bookseller waits to discover which customer this customer is. The customer is looking for a particular book but unfortunately the bookseller cannot make out the words over the drone of Swan Lake. The bookseller apologises, indicates the sign, asks if it would be possible for the customer to write the title of the book down. Only the customer appears not to know the title. The bookseller begins to search relevant terms on the database, hoping that the book will surface. The orchestra tunes up. The customer drums their nails on the desk in time with the first violin. The bookseller asks if there is another title by the author that the customer could name. The customer makes some guesses. The fifth bar ends halfway through. The customer looks over at their children, their nails still drumming on the desk. The bookseller can only find books in French by that author, and they are not available to order. The customer says the book is really good. The bookseller does not say sorry, my mistake, I was looking for a bad book. The bookseller is suddenly quite hot, perhaps because she is still sitting on the radiator, and the soup was very hot, and her tongue is very sore and furry-feeling. The orchestra is warming up. One of the children presses the button again, then again, hammering their finger on the book like a woodpecker. The bookseller says I am sorry but I just can't find it. The orchestra's warming up becomes one interminable flatline. The bookseller notices that the child has lifted its finger off the book and yet the sound continues. The bookseller is not sure if the sound is coming from the book or from within her own head. The children have walked away from the book and are hanging about by the door. They are exhibiting symptoms of guilt. As the bookseller notices this, the customer looks at the sign and says, in the voice the bookseller uses to talk to her GP, is there anyone else I can speak to?

The bookseller's anger is not the customer's fault. Emotions are subjective experiences. The sign says

SIGN SEVEN

CLOSED

(in red)

PART 2

✠

POETRY

LAURA CELESTE

The Radium Girls

Paintbrush, radium, dip.
Paintbrush, radium, lip.

Lick the hairs to a fine tip
& paint the tiny numbers

on the dial from 1 to 12.
Each worker *ticks, ticks, ticks*.

A watch equals less than a cent.
A girl equals less than a watch.

Gums leak red oil. Teeth
fall out like loose screws.

Rot-riddled jaws snap
from springs & corrode into dust.

More, the boss instructs.
It's safe. Stop making a fuss.

He hushes the girls
when they ask for a review,

pays a doctor to report:
whores, sick with syphilis.

The girls' faces glow lime green.
Bones screech like wheels.

No one knows how many
rotations the girls have left.

As they stand up to testify
in court against American Radium,

their breaths count down,
their words reverberate —

over the wireless, in the papers,
across the states, into the decades.

KIRSTIE MILLAR

Hard Worker

1.

My job is hard and I do not understand it *oh how nice it must be to have a job you don't understand!* the customers say and I want to slap them and say *what do you know of my hard work what do you know of my suffering!* but I smile and say *can I get you anything?* my job is boring and I understand that it is my job to be bored to be nice to people to say *hello* and *welcome* and *I won't be a moment* and *can I assist you with anything?* my job is to circle back my job is to write emails my job is stupid I hate my job but every morning I wake up and wash my face every morning I vomit sour sick into the sink and rinse it down with cold water every morning I shake with fear my boss will be mean to me maybe today is the day my boss will be cruel and will mean it but I am cruel too and devilish

2.

Your mother works too hard my grandmother said and she knew what hard work meant her hands like blue prunes when they should have been sunlight her hands hard when they should have been the moon her hands cool against my face that time I had a fever I imagined me nestling inside my mother and my mother nestling inside my grandmother while she worked at the factory sewing gowns for the women up the hill and far away from the gurgling black smoke my mother nestled inside her belly round like the moon and me

glimmering inside my mother's egg like a pearl and my grandmother
on her knees scrubbing floors at the hospital while me and my mother
played like fish but the doctors could be cruel as well you know

3.

My mother was working at the hotel when she found the man's
dead body it was summer and she hadn't seen the man for a few
days so she just had a feeling and her boss said *it's a good thing you
checked in this heat he would have melted into the floor that would have
been expensive to clean up* but did her boss send her home after the
ambulance took the man away beneath the black shroud for weeks
she had dreams of the dead body which was grey like an alien moon
my mother couldn't walk past his room without crying but someone
had to deliver the post and refill the ice machine and once when she
passed by the room the man's voice said her name soft just a flutter
against the ear was the ghost of the man thanking her for finding
him and did her boss send her home to us with full pay or did she
finish out her shift I can't remember

4.

I am a bad worker because I use too many sick days because I am
not resilient enough because I am not a self-starter enough because
I lack the motivation to get better did you know that my body has
been sliced open in twenty places? the wounds struggle to heal and
once my boss grew angry when I cancelled my shift after my incision
wept and howled the pink crescent scar ripping like tissue paper
my organs all stuck together as I sit at my desk and take codeine
and today my boss is angry with me because a cyst bloomed on

my ovary and twisted and turned bad and split oh god the riotous
pain but I try to be patient with my boss who regrets hiring me
because I am sick and I am devilish after Disease pointed his long
blue finger at me as I type on my keyboard my eye burns a vessel
ruptures blood fills the milky white opal my eye becomes a blood
moon my eye becomes a cherry my eye becomes a howling mouth
my ovary shudders and blinks my body is disobedient and hurting
but do I have any sick days left I can't remember I can't remember

NAOMI MORRIS

Produce Valuable Work

I have constructed a doppelganger: she
concentrates for longer and reads more.
She completes chores without excess
thought or feeling. The usual contours
of life are not disruptive:
getting dressed   doing the washing up   making food   going outside.
These she does not find hard or new
or novel, every time.

She has time to sharpen
every knifeline of prose because, I believe,
she does not possess the brash and humiliating
need to communicate a feeling.
She spends her reserves crafting word by word,
so that her attempts at (successful) communication
are never embarrassing or misconstrued.

I am thinking about how the knifelines of pain
along my neck and shoulders
doesn't affect her. She does not feel
them. She can sit all day at a desk.
Then counteract this sitting not with more sitting (lying)
but with supple stretches before a run
or other physical activity.

Her unfeeling is not numbness to everything.
she feels what you are supposed to feel:
the thrill of intellectual stimulation, the gentle
dread of occasional existential questions, spots
of ennui and longing that feed into and produce valuable
work.

SUSAN L. LIN

Balancing Act

The Human Animal is on display
whenever she mounts the stage:
Spectators below have paid $5
to watch her repertoire of tricks:
a pirouette, a side aerial, an arabesque, a split leap,
a bow.

Before she finishes her routine,
the curtain falls,
bringing an abrupt end
to the show. Soon,

she's the one who must pay
for other human animals
to examine her body more closely,
explain why
she can no longer perform all those moves
that were once second nature.
She offers them a $5 bill,
but that won't cover it—
the final cost will be astronomical.

Black Mirror

The Human Animal has somehow ended up
on a mailing list for piano collectors.
In the post, she receives envelopes
from local universities, operas, and private dealers.
Major Liquidation! Every piano in our inventory
must be sold immediately! the flyers proclaim.
She played the instrument a long time ago,
doesn't understand why the promise of their song
now haunts her like that of winged species.

'Piano Sale / *Details inside...*'
Another envelope is decidedly more coy, employing
the kind of tantalizing promise that must make
piano lovers everywhere start salivating.
The onyx-colored model from her childhood
living room had a hinged lid on top;
she would sometimes open it up
to inspect the musical instrument's anatomy,
watch the tiny hammers hit the vertical strings.
An intricate mechanism that reminded her
of a wind-up bird.

She once saw a pale ghost in a music shop;
it looked more like sculpted white chocolate.
But in her home piano, she witnessed her image
reflected on every shiny black surface
when she removed sheet music
from the fold-out shelf.

The sudden appearance of a girl's face
made her jump: She was always surprised
to find The Human Animal was still alive.

Fairy Tale Endings

The Human Animal is a blurry shape
projected onto the blank wall,
a head that won't stop rolling.
She is a shadow. She is a spy.
She could be a real human animal
if she were filled to the rim of her cup
with softer cloud-like thoughts,
emptied of the magic poisons
and dangerous potions that keep her young.

She is a dance because human animals
are all the intangibles we love.
She is a strand of hair because human animals
are all the extensions that fail us,
and once upon a time, she crumpled to the floor
like an unwanted page of words.
She is a girl patiently falling, forever waiting
to land in her final resting place.
But she also transforms into a cracked eggshell
whenever she collides with figures from the past
who yearn to write a fictional future.

The truth is more simple:
No matter what anyone says, she will always be
a human animal.

CARRIE SEAR

PIP

i spoke to God over the phone and asked Him for pocket money,
a 'please Sir' plea. in a letter, He said

> *Tell me how your health condition or disability affects you.*

i crawled to the window and shouted my National Insurance number
palms up like a soup bowl, non-threatening, polite. sub_____.

                                                    human
                                                    missive
                                                    par

Dave, the representative, said

> *Name it. Prove it. Sign it off three times and sit. Tongue out.*
> *Tell me how often you crawl, when you fall, how you fail.*
> *Gut yourself and hand them over for the deserving.*

i obeyed. he was God's agent. God's decommissioned paramedic,
the guardian angel Dave. knees to soil, i wept my medication list.

i wasn't God's problem anymore. i was Dave's problem.
to me, he said

> *That sounds very hard. It must be difficult. Tell me more,*
> *about these problems you have.*

i kept on digging my pit, soil nails and blanket nausea.
above the pit, Dave's report was engraved:

No falls in the bathroom, so –
Passed her driving test, so –
Uses standard cutlery, so –

KEEV Ó BAOILL

I do go to the dentist

In the evening, my flatmate crawls out from their room
            in the basement

            I too emerge, but from upstairs, making my way down
the narrowing steps

What is there left for us to say?

            She tells me, vaguely, of her fears — about employment,
application deadline and application deadline and application
deadline and loss. Oh, and loss.
                              I do not respond in tow

I worry I may never find a job, I worry I am useless, I worry I am
useless and I have no purpose, I worry I may never find a job I worry
I am useless I worry I am useless I worry I am useless I worry I have
no purpose

I try to handwrite poems — you tell me there is something special,
something particular, about putting pen to paper.
                              I do not, discernibly,
agree with you

I start to handwrite poems, my poems,
                  only the drafts,

and it does work
There is something to it

And yet,

    my hand begins to ache,
    not quite through the tips of my fingers, rough and clumsy
    as they are, but deeper, right
    down to the flesh-mound atop my wrist

And further, further
further still — I hone in

Soft and unrelenting, searing in its companionship,
        talking reams of my self-flagellation.

*   I should go to the gym,*
*   I should build more muscle, I should,*
*   I should do my physio, I should, I should*
*   I should go to the gym*

It tenses, that fleshy mound, pulsing down my outer arm, my
forearm, teasing, vice-like, at the elbow. And yet, as I lay my pen
down, it teases through my limbic

                l i m b i c s,

my miniature limbs! my fingers,
haunting through the tip
    relaying back to Mr Elbow,

They tell me writing is my job. I am a poet.
        I try to internalise that what Kae Tempest spoke
unto me, *On Connections*
        when I began getting paid to write poems

But I do write poems, and they are poorly
Just like I were. They are poorly poems. They are poems that lack
conviction. Convictions. Plural. They are poems, they are poems.

I do not go to the doctor:
      Not when, bit by bit, I begin to fall apart — Why do they call it
that? To "fall apart" I am not to fall apart, I am freezing up, I am
calcifying at the root

I do not go to the doctor,
not when I have a growing-pain across my chest, or, when,
I begin to notice, increasingly so, small pin-prick dots, in
their droves, red and

                  spotted about,

I do not go to the doctor, when, a friendly floater begins
to spread its wispy legs across
my retina,

            nor when their wispy nature grows ever more robust
                              I do not go to the doctor,
                              I do not go to the doctor.

I do go to the dentist
      I do go to the dentist, and I do have her check my teeth

I do go to the dentist to feel her poke and prod, taut and damming
against my gums, I do have her feel around, latex-gloved and
rubbered as she is, her plastic limbic appendages protruding
as
they are around my lubricated tissues. I concentrate on the mound of
my gums as they relent against her carefully positioned seals

I concentrate as she explains the purpose of a dental dam
to me,
step-by-step, so as not to
rattle
my
senses

I do not tell her that I already know what a dental dam is, nor do i
tell her how inexhaustive her list is
I do go to the dentist, but i do not tell her when the
abscess beneath my gum line grows, enraged

I do go to the dentist but I do not tell her when her lidocaine
does not work to numb out her drill, nor my screeching nerves,
I do not tell her about the faulty collagen, the bendy joints, like warm
plastic left to contort in the rain, nor the fragility of it all

I do not protest as she soothes me, as she tells me how i
cannot possibly
feel the withering, searing distress of her drill
I do not disagree when she reminds me, again, *not
to worry,*
how it might be *a bit* uncomfortable, but that there
is *never any pain*

I do not argue as she rushes to fill the hole left
in my jaw, as she bores away at the corrosion,
her rush-job excavation,

I do not tell her, I do not tell her

I do go to the dentist

Fox Tails

I have caught crows on my tongue. They prophesied in subsongs — a fuse of hoarse coos, caws, rattles, and clicks that conveyed a cautionary note with a hint of luck on the tail end of the message. Death overhangs each day; seldom does it swoop down within a mere countdown of seconds.

As a suffer of GAD, I was told to wash my hair with baked oat meal. The natural scrub releases trauma from the back of the mind, where it filters through the hair follicles. Once detached, the pervasive root issue falls away. With eyes closed, I listened to the water drain away together with the putrefaction, captured in the quietude of a deep sigh.

We need not tolerate the rooster. You will see him masquerading as a party balloon filled with glittering images and sounds. If it's tossed at you now and again, don't catch it. You cannot make a cock wear shoes to walk an apology out of his coup on the sound of cock-a-doodle-do. We cannot make fake eggs fertile.

I see Mary, who also has GAD, playing an axe like a ukulele while singing by the decorative wire meshing around the coup. Every time the cock goes near her, she stops playing to whet her instrument on stone. Her song becomes a flurry of sharp, harsh sounds — marginalia written during storms. As the lightning struck, she breathed in the fire.

When tired, Mary sleeps alone in a quart basket on a bed of road maps and covers herself with four russet-coloured fox tails. Here, she feels cradled and shrinks to the size of a pea. In a dream, she drives a beaten-up truck with a screwdriver wrenched into the ignition.

Advice Needed

In a dance in the skies, a high-wire artist leans on air. His confidence
is almost unforgivable; it's a sting in the gut with a 30-mm-
thick cable. Defiant strides implement rotational inertia, light with
intent, they forge ahead. His hair tickles the acidic, smog-filled
cloud with unprecedented rapidity.

I imagine the balancing pole being vertical and curving at the top
into a shepherd's staff or a question mark. Words spin out of the hook:
mankind, womankind. Do you mind the mind of humankind?
Divinity, truth, and love — are we down with or considering love
and truth? The prick: a genuine message is a message with a question
that needs a genuine answer.

The insight into the impenetrable remains obscure and aloof;
I need more air to breathe. Like the tightrope walker who dreams
of a world without ground and high winds. Funambulism is not for
me; I don't want to become hazy, vertigo drunk, and fall with
a splash of entrails.

So, should I build a perch or a viewing platform of twigs and stones
with a mattress of hay underneath? Being careful. Will it bring me
closer to knowing without being fractured even more? I won't allow
any wishy-washiness or 'ritual steeling'.
Man soll den Tag nicht vor dem Abend loben.
I will embrace the novel, not the entangled marsh of webs open to suggestion.
Laconic verse will do, repetition is acceptable if it brings results.

Burgundy

I like the colour burgundy; it exudes a blood-warming magic that lifts. Each morning, wake up to the sight of three powerful energy givers: my paintings, *Cosmic Mechanisms, An Epiphany #2*, and *The Celestial Walk,* two of which are framed with an inch of lake mint green. I want to dive into the warm, thick swirls of liquorice burgundy and swim in its unique, reassuring presence. A secure prenatal state that is quiet and protective. GAD will disappear along with its troubled sling.

The quietude of Burgundy is free of spite, noise, smell, and anxiety, making it the perfect place for the miracle of gestation. On a sultry summer's evening, a vigneron makes a toast with a glass of Burgundy to pay homage to the *terroir*, which is the synergy of grapes, earth, weather, winery, and human touch. A paragon of sophistication, it doesn't care about the status quo.

In sleep, the burgundy land subsides, but not completely. Dreams are home to angelic states, and swallows rejoice in murmuration. I ascend a filigree, cast-iron staircase to a plateau of deep burgundy soil and press a cheek into its form. I know that life is there to be lived.

Slow down / Ṣẹ jẹ jẹ (2023)

Slow downnnnn

I need you to consider self, I need you to consider wealth, I need you to consider your mind

Rest your bones, sit them down, normalise the ability to prioritise
Tell yourself
Worthy am I!
Worthy am I!

Slow downnnnn

Get up from the table, actually, go and rest, don't sit down past 8, past 9, past 10, 11, 1..........and not rest

I need you to slow down. I don't care what it is, I just need you to slow down

We need you. Remember long after you are gone we will be fine, but you need you.
You need you for needing sake, you need you for surviving for your sake
You need you for thriving sake, you need you for loving sake, you need you for legacy sake.

You need you and we need you, but the need that we need of you can only be needed if you are here to need you. If you are here to fight for you.

And the fight is not in loudness and banging of feet and swaying of hands telling you to go to bed or trying to manipulate you for a spa treatment or for you to try this new healthy snack, no it's not that. The fight is in slow-paced resistance to your normalisation of maladapted rest, to your normalisation of not chilling, your waka waka, waka waka, waka waka! That's often too much for your own good.

I need you to slow down
I need you to actually just fucking slow down

I need you to sometimes grab that tea, put feet up and lay down. I need you to sometimes not even grab tea because sometimes tea has too much caffeine and I need you to just go to bed and sleep. And sometimes I need you to switch on the tele and watch something, not because you are interested in the stories of the protagonist, but because you need to take your mind away from your life and put your mind on the lives of mythical creatures and fictional characters; things that do not exist but excite. Things that do not exist but excite and take mind, body and spirit far away....

I need you for momentary chill, for momentary pace of chilling.... decompress

I need you to just freaking slow down, I need you to be golden, slow down for rejuvenation, slow down for pacing, slow down for your own libation, in the living.

I need you to slow down

I need you to wake up the next morning, not seeing tired eyes but your skin is glowing

It's glowing from rest, it's not glowing from shaggs, it's glowing from rest.

Nobody knocked your back out my dear, you actually got rest.

Nobody was tugging you and moving your arms side to side and lifting your legs to say 'baby just one round.' No you actually rested!

You actually took the time to prioritise your sleep, you took the time to say nah not this time, I'm good.

Sleep on that side, I'll sleep on this side.

Now you're actually taking the time to just skip on paddles and not on bones.

You're drooling, your lips are droollllllllllllling, they're drooling.

You wake up and there's a white scar just down your chin, because you've gone to lala land.

Ah! My dear, you're enjoying O!, enjoyment, enjoy—ment.

That's good, I want more of it!

I want lackadaisical days in dreamyland for you and I want you to be so engrossed in your sleep that omo! oofe ji, olati ji… but ofe ji..

Mennn it's so nice to breathe in rejuvenation and say, 'Omo! I feel soft and pampered', without anyone touching my body, without any treatment or this or that, I just needed sleep, I needed to slow the fuck down, I needed to stop doing this and that and the third.. unproductive tidings for the sake of motion. I need to tell myself to slow down because I needed that shit

Thank you for talking some sense into me because I needed that shit
Thank you for holding me down because I needed that shit
It's something else and I can't really explain it but I needed that shit

I'm slowing down, I'm slowing down, I'm slowing down... I am
slowing down

Wà
Asíkò è tí de,
Ma rò pupò
Séjèjè

Come
Your time is now
Relax, don't think too much
Take it easy

Monthly Woes (2023)

Hollow baths stayed in for its clinical cold, spine will reach out to edges for comfort and lounge till it is so.

Legs spread while clenching tunnels as it wilts and breathes again and again.

Womb sore, arches sore, flesh sore, all are sore.

Body fit be stronger as it dey run dis ting regular

Body fit strong as it dey run dis ting regular

Dulling with yellow salves that leave the deepest stings and

penetrate far through the existence of aches.

Chai! Aboniki you are god here

A million legs runneth through fibres, as they scatter they bring these cuttings, sharp, blistering, like bubbles with spirit being pumped; expanding inside till they're content.

In moments of popping, hissing away the fragments of air that consume your insides, a thin rod inserts itself in piercing through until it wants to stop. It quite enjoys this.

Falling, crouching, standing, crawling, lingering and gasping for a steady pace and air, until ready to returnto former moments. Esu!

Streams of pink viscous, chunky strands, clumps, clots will run away down drain and do it over again.

As they exit warm walls, there are reconciliations of hands and toes, love and woes of a being never quite manifested. A loss in a way of a little one who never got to call you Mama.

Maybe relief, maybe joy, maybe this is grace
But next month fit bring another one.

Oro yi kpo

Relief

Pain

Babies

Horniness

Tiredness

PART 3

✠

NON-
FICTION

A Victorian Timepiece

ELSPETH WALKER

Tight chested I sit in bed, at desks or in moments when no one is looking. I have become a mouth breather, a lilac under-eyed woman, I now indulge in long skirts and dresses: I have become a Victorian relic.

It started with a whooping cough, but not in the cradle like most get it. Instead I was twenty-one, supposedly young, invincible, and most of all healthy. The ninety day cough, as it is sometimes called, lasted in my body for five months officially, but it's now been nearly six years of over tired and overworked lungs. It lasted longer because, alongside being young and naive, I was in a lower socioeconomic band and working zero-hour contracts as I finished my final year of university.

Nothing screams poor house like whooping cough at twenty-one, we would joke in my family. Jokes make the unbelievable easier to manage, to put in a box and say what was that? So glad it's over. It's easier than saying if only I didn't have to keep working, if only I wasn't at a rich intake university, serving up pints and pub food, spending thirteen hours on campus between the library and paid work. If only I didn't look like a grubby stereotype of sickly poor.

The cough comes with a unique and specific sound. There is a gasp with a whistle or hooting element to it. You cough air out frantically, painfully, and then inhale it back violently. Neither one feels like you're breathing. Associated with workhouses, an old age ailment, one that can kill babies, like a twisted sitcom, I got it during my so-called youthful years. When they finally tested me for the right thing, I received a letter asking me to stay away from children, babies, and older people (this was a year before 'vulnerable groups' was a common term). By that time I was already very pale, the thinnest I had been, and probably ever will be, my face looked gaunt across my cheeks, my back ached and my teeth suffered from the vomiting after constant coughing fits.

That period was bad, and then it slowly faded. I could walk longer distances without becoming lethargic, no more sounds when coughing, and, finally, I looked less like a ghost haunting the pub I worked at. What lingers however is the reality of history repeating itself, of the lack of real choice to say no to work meaning I didn't really recover properly, and now I live like a steeplechase between chest infections.

There is a bitter irony from this cycle of labour: to earn enough to get by comfortably I work at the burn-out level, which causes me to be run down, which causes chest infections in my weak lungs, which means I have to call in sick, which means I earn less, which means I must work more to compensate. There is also the reality of people in lower socioeconomic groups ending up in more precarious contracts, with lower pay. In the arts it is often called freelance which is coded for zero-hours contract, which means if I call in sick I won't get paid. At times, it feels like this is where my brain ignores my body. It says you can push yourself. You have Thursday off, recover then. As if the body worked like the machine piece they wanted.

So I think of myself as a Victorian woman. Coughing and curled in on herself, churning out work because one day it will be enough. I often see time as a luxury, a commodity I was not born with a surplus of. I spend most of my life chasing to have it, so that when I finally grasp some, all I can do is sleep through it. Breathe through vapour inhalers, chase around doctors, try the newest chest medicine, so it doesn't feel so miserable. I wish to be a renaissance woman on a chaise longue, letting time heal me as I bask serenely. Instead, I feel like an etching in an old textbook of a woman sitting in a musty room slowly rotting from the stagnant pools in her chest.

I want to see each lung, to hold and nurture them, but most of the time I swear and curse at them, as if it was their choice, they are the problem, not the cycle of unending unrest.

Inside it feels like two veiny dry slabs of meat are dangling. There is a bruise like ache where they pull on my chest. I'm in my mid-twenties now, and when an infection comes (they always come) I get out of breath walking to the bus. The meat seems to pull tight as I sit at a desk. If I lie down I will only fall into a sweaty sleep. I imagine something inside of me is putting up scaffolding, trying to brace and help support my lungs, yet it seems like a losing battle. Either way, it demands I sleep through days, go to the loo at work for a power nap, or alternatively over indulge with coffee in an attempt to replace lost sleep.

Having to stay static means the brain is either over-working or flatlined. There is no middle. I begin to feel more like a robot going through the cyclical motions, time measured by my lungs and their infections. I think about how it must seem, to be young and look like an old image of a wretched woman. I'm not sure I was ever meant to be out of this cycle. That the need for work ensures I keep becoming a creature who has to work. I have become a relic, a monument to the history of working women in England who get sick but are shamed or unable to take sick days, I have become a Victorian timepiece.

ELSPETH WALKER

Feline Friendly

HATTY NESTOR

Something moved between us. It was okay. It was okay because it had to be, because in that twilight moment, the world telescoped. I needed to reach towards something I couldn't quite grasp. Relating is beautiful and strange. Communion is a rare reciprocality. She knows the strangeness of illness, the flat planes of mundanity. She has always been inside.

Care came as a cat again – in the beginning lighthearted and sincere. I felt surer of this connection and love than at any other time in my life. The bed became a sanctuary. A church. A something. Light was shining through. Darkness was arising. The feeling of good health is emerging. I should feel terror but don't. Most disarming over Christmas when stakes are high.

Sometimes you read a story, watch a movie or walk down the street and somebody is going against the grain. They're fucking with time. I'm trying to fuck with time. My body's time. Alison Kafer writes about how crip time bends the clock to meet disabled bodies and minds. But it also distorts interrelations, interdependence, and expectation. Crip fucking time. Time is fucking me up. Immersed in this crip time, your body, despite being the source of suffering, is your only companion – your enemy and comfort. This double bind remerges as a strange boundary between intimacy and kindness, limitation and control. It's not even control. It's patterns. It is never quite like that when you're sick. Assume the ambiguity. To share the unknown is the greatest solace.

The truth is I just feel terrible. Things hurt. Nerves shoot, synapses across the brain. And I don't know when it'll end, because the idea of an end is actually the place of mourning. An early death! Fucking hell it's hard to think. Back to Christmas. I am told that the cat is clinically 'overweight', has bunions on her tail, and first-stage cancer. She takes little pills, pink ones, to get through the day. We both do, mine are blue though. The bunions repulse me, but I feel them, up and down with my hands. Bumps like anal beads. Her belly drags along the floor, a strange mop. Big flop. It's all confused. She groans. We are both in a limbo state. An elsewhere state. Something else states. We are morphing and contouring in the bed the boundary between self/other becomes somewhat blurry. The cat conducts the bed; she orchestrates.

Sometimes I feel I could die without the cat. Persist, persist. That death would take a small bite. She understands my body as a strange system of unpredictability. Her name has changed multiple times, and she even went through a period of just being called the cat. I would lay with her, next to her, synergies colliding. In her body I saw my own, failing, in pain, unable to function, a disappointment. And embarrassment, a source of constant confusion.

The morning is clear, still. This is our lived reality, the fantasy of the other. Something like feline fury and fever dreams of forever. We are empathising. I felt very loving.

I felt good. Felt the weight of it all and sat amongst it, leaned into it. Fluctuated between thought and feeling.

Desert air and hues of pink sky, grazing this limbo state. Clouds don't form because there are none, the desire for resolution smoulders into a hazy entrapment. We are here. The desire to give myself a shape, a parameter, persists. Yet I am undone and remade. The cat is now dying. She is dead. Limber. This grave body has ignited life. It's all ours.

Burn

REBECCA COXON

I am filming paramedics for a television documentary series. We are sitting in a static ambulance, grabbing a quick lunch before heading off to another urgent job. Every job is urgent, of course, when you're driving an ambulance. Falafel wrap and tea for me. I am holding the hot tea in a polystyrene cup. The wispy steam screams danger so I carefully place it in between my legs. It will be sturdier there as we start driving again. I look down and the cup is gone. Split. Shit. The tea seeps through my black jeans in slow motion, along my thighs, into my groin. Everything is scalding wet. I try not to make a noise but it's impossible. The paramedics turn around in their front seats and stare, then sigh. They ask if I'm okay and continue nibbling their sandwiches. I roll my eyes internally. I am embarrassed. *Idiot.* These will take ages to dry.

We drive away, but now my legs are getting hotter, not cooler. Shame pulses into pain; the kind that makes passing out preferable. The paramedics urge me to remove my jeans and I do so, reluctantly. I'm at work, how humiliating. I feel like a toddler being told to undress by their parents. What underwear am I even wearing? I peel back the sodden layer of denim and my freshly seared legs are exposed to the daylight. Craters of yellow; half-peeled tangerine texture. The surface of another planet. Still silently blistering my skin. I didn't know skin could bubble.

You've got to be kidding me. We are supposed to be saving other people's lives, not injuring ourselves. The polite, but irked, paramedics throw cold gel packs at me and drive us to the nearest A&E. I was laughing with them a few minutes ago but now I cannot hold a conversation, or finish a thought. The pain is unbearable. *From a cup of fucking tea.*

I am angry at myself for this forced detour. They should be saving lives or scooping up old ladies off the floor, not faffing about with me. By the time we arrive at the A&E doors the pain has evaporated. I can only assume the nerve endings have burnt off.

Saline drip, the doctor suggests. Second degree burns.

'How did it happen?' they ask.

'A cup of tea,' I reply, sheepishly.

'You'd be surprised how common it is!' They are kind, and I am grateful.

'We're going to need to photograph your private parts, is that okay?'

'I guess so,' I reply, hoping it wouldn't come to this.

'Could you pop off your underwear?'

A tired digital camera appears, it looks like something we took on nights out in 2009. NHS budget cuts, no doubt. Click. Click. They photograph me from angles I've never been photographed before and email them to a 'specialist burns unit'. My frothy thighs and singed vulva exist somewhere in the ether now. I am to visit the Chelsea and Westminster Burns Unit in the morning, they say. They patch me up and I am home by midnight.

Nine hours later I am trekking across London, from East to West, thigh dressings chafing. I am greeted by some lovely nurses who specialise in scorched skin. They want to do something called 'de-roofing'.

'Have you taken a paracetamol this morning?' they ask.

But no one told me to take any painkillers. It's too late now. They scrape away the top layer of crust from each blister with little scalpels, etching pain back into my skin like a lino print.

Intentional rupture, removing dead tissue, reducing infection.

I go back to work immediately after.

Exactly a year earlier I was in hospital having laparoscopy surgery for endometriosis. Widespread across my bladder, bowels and womb, the surgeon said. It explained my burning pelvis symptoms. So they cauterised my insides. Now I've accidentally burned my outsides. *How can burning be the problem and the answer?*

Three years later and my burns have healed but my brain is sick instead. I can't feel anything. My job is making me ill. I cannot get pregnant. I am burnt out with a big 'B' and a massive 'Ohh'. I have the slow but certain understanding that my feelings don't matter any more – to my boyfriend or my boss – so I stop having them. My spirit is snuffed out.

It's probably best that my emotions are cauterised too, I reason, lest they cause me to jump off a balcony at my own birthday party again and ruin everyone's evening. These days I'm relying on tarot cards for guidance and horoscopes for hope. It's not even a secret anymore. I bring pretty-coloured cards to social events and watch my friends lean in closer as I relay their futures and they pretend not to worry about me.

Anhedonia;
inability to feel pleasure in normally pleasurable activities.

I feel pitted like an olive, aching for its lost seed. Did I ever even have one? I have forgotten now. Don't bite or swallow, you must delicately nibble around it. Like you do in work meetings. Like you do with conversations about children. You must avoid it, respect it, then spit it out.

It's the hesitation when a colleague asks 'How are you?' and the split-second between lying (Fine, thanks) or being honest (I am depressed and don't find joy in anything).

All whilst hoisting a heavy smile with withering string. They don't notice your dead-eyes or your soul-cold curt comments. They think they are ironic *hahaha* – and they can't afford to lose you. But you've both walked away now anyway; back to your desks.

Burns, they can see. Bubbling skin is serious.

'Does it hurt? Go home, get it checked out. Don't come in.'

A blistered brain is lazy, awkward, inconvenient.

'Yes it did hurt. No it doesn't anymore. I don't feel anything anymore.'

It is the burden of being burdenless, as my brother once said. But really the burden is my brain. I imagine clicking it back into place like I do my knuckles and toes and neck. Crack. Just need to get the angle and alignment right and it will feel better. Crack.

Cavitation;
when a synovial joint expands rapidly to allow dissipation of gases within.

I google
is anyone actually happy
for the third time this week. It feels like the most rational thing to do. Like someone will just explain that it's normal to feel this confused and disoriented inside my dull pressurised

head and say there's nothing you can do about it just keep typing and nodding and trying.

There are no answers, just an abomination of questions. There is luck and grief and laughter and child abuse. All mixed up together. That's human nature. It can't be helped. My work day (making serious documentaries) is full of it, dripping with it, saturated with all the human suffering, and goodness too. We're trying to help, but we're not really. We are showing, not doing.

Tears glut in my throat, but not at the sad stuff anymore. I'm thoroughly numbed to all that. The good stuff too, that's why there is no fun anymore. I swallow it all down, go home and watch the way my cat has a secret set of eyelids when he dreams.

I wish I had them too. Another layer to shield us from seeing. Maybe I wouldn't have so many nightmares about falling.

I watch youtube videos and try to tempt fate into giving me another life.

Manifest, Gemini.

I wonder if you can will life into this world, into your body.

I drink raw cacao and naked-float in a salt tank that tries to take me back to the womb, but I find myself suspended in a swell of worry instead. Anx-i-ous thought-s bob-bing a-round acc-i-dent-ally touch-ing them with my fing-er-tips and sink-ing in-to guilt a-gain. Itching, dry, salt skin belly.

The womb I grew in was full anyway. That's how it is with triplets: chock-a-block. Just enough room at the inn. Four failed attempts at IVF, then three at once. Imagine.

My sensible body has numbed itself. As a child I fainted a lot. Classroom, doctor's office, beach, bathroom floor, kitchen floor, shop floor. Vaccines, heat, a teacher's rage, a sliced finger, a new piercing, my sister's foot, giving blood.

Several times I banged my head. But even the floor can't save you. Once, alone in a public toilet cubicle, I recognised the familiar woozy whirling and sat down on the cold tile floor. But I still woke up with a headache and a giant lump. My body had still fallen.

How can I stop falling while I'm unconscious?

A violet boulder bloomed out the brow of my skull. A foreign object from under my skin. I was on my way to work so they sent me to A&E, they needed to be covered for insurance purposes. At least it was a language they could understand.

Sometimes the original injury is overshadowed by our involuntary reaction to it. Our brain is only trying to help but it ends up making things worse. Falling, fainting, switching off, going numb.

Depression is like winning a game of shooting yourself in the foot, then looking around and realising you have no limbs left. *But at least you're winning at something.*

I start having vivid Sertraline dreams. I wonder why and when my entire life became *italicised. When did living inside my head become the default setting? How do I get out of here. Questions without question marks any more; just facts, ampersands, aeons, periods, full stops. Forever stuck in this round box with a breathing hole.*

I stop drinking because it's the only time my anger flares up. A liquid ignition, doused over myself, spitting flames all over my friends and lovers. A flickering orange rage. For a few hours nothing can put it out. It is, eventually, only tempered down by an overruling, isolating, obliterating sadness. I used to wake up dehydrated, thirsty with shame and regret. Now I wake up feeling calm but empty.

The scars on my inner thighs are very faint now, I don't

even notice them. But I am careful around tea, and adamant that polystyrene cups should come with a warning.

I don't have a baby and I quit my job. There is still fire in my belly.

Matisse in bed

STEPH ROBERTS

A photograph, black and white: an artist – male, white – propped up in bed with a pillow, a tartan blanket over his legs. He is drawing on the wall with a brush attached to an extended stick, about 5 feet long. He is balding, with a beard; owlish glasses. Looming behind his left shoulder, in the space between his bed and the wall is a large wooden cross.

I too – art curator, female, white – am propped up in my own bed, a knitted blanket over my legs, scrolling through the comments on my phone.

» So inspiring!

» This is amazinggg

» Where the will is the way is found

» Lazy AF

They all annoy me.

The inspiration porn – the distrust of access aids – the secret suspicion of laziness (always, the laziness).

A charge is created when disabled bodies are seen working,

doing, making. Reactions are diverse, but never neutral – even the seemingly innocuous ones.

Even here, with Henri Matisse, disabled and at the top of his game, working on his self-proclaimed masterpiece: the design for the interior of the *Chapelle du Rosaire* in Vence, the south of France.

A cancer diagnosis at the age of 72 and a series of operations had changed the course of the last decade of Matisse's life. He had bouts of severe ill health, long periods of recuperation, and was left with long-term mobility issues. He became a wheelchair user, and often worked from bed.

(» Lazy AF)

In the photograph, Matisse is painting a circle with a shape like the number 7 in the middle. It's the rudimentary beginnings of a face, but looks a bit like a clock, hands pointing half-past nine. Also on the wall are two saintly figures painted in loose, cascading lines; and near the foot of his bed, a series of geometric painted patterns arranged in grid-like boxes.

To his left, in the gap between the bed and the wall, is a ladder: perhaps an aid to help him reach the highest parts of the wall. Next to the ladder, a cross. An overhead lamp is strapped to it like a strange angular Christ, a Rosary string hanging from it like a beaded trail of blood.

Across his lap is a makeshift table, cluttered with bric-a-brac and paper and books. I study his set-up – his objects artfully arranged, all within easy reach around him.

In *Henri Matisse: A Second Life* Alastair Sooke explains how after his surgery, which both saved and almost killed him, Matisse found a rebirth of sorts; a period of renewed creativity and drive, which the artist himself called a 'second life'. Sooke describes how Matisse 'returned from the grave' for a final creative flourish which topped his already stellar career. Struggling with his usual ways of working, he started to experiment with less physically demanding techniques. This led to his famous 'cut-out' phase, where he used scissors and paper to create colourful, bold collages. He worked as and when he could, even from bed.

In the first year of my chronic illness, my world folded in on itself with an uncompromising swiftness, reduced right down until my life was contained entirely in the space of a queen size mattress. Matisse is known for his fondness of women on mattresses. His exoticised figures recline seductively against pillows, usually with one, sometimes two, of their breasts hanging out – a white man's Orientalist fantasy. But I doubt Matisse would have wanted to paint me reclining on my bed. I was

sick:
violently, gruesomely sick. For months my body leaked and burnt and bled into sheet and foam *skin-shed blood-slick stick* my bed both coffin and cot

I was
born anew / had never
felt so close to death

I spent entire months in bed, surviving in my cocoon of blankets, with occasional trips to the living room settee.

I would curl and contract under throws, rock myself gently to distract from the pain, slipping in and out of sleep when it chose to visit me. Consciousness came in a dreamy drifting haze between ceiling-cracks and cobwebs, slanted shadows and lights. The world outside a distant muffle, or the sharply focused sting of an Instagram scroll glowing beneath bedcovers.

Too bright, too loud.

I became a bed-dweller. My needs felt monstrous in my new mattressed isolation.

> **Bed-dwelling.** *There is no limit to my bodily wants. It moves beyond boundaries, scribbles outside its lines. I want to fly like crow. My arms stretch, but the stuckness of my flesh pulls me down. I am not crow. I have fingers that scratch, and legs that bleed. I am land-bound, bed-bound, tethered to this room. I dream in feather-claws, scream in clouds. I want to swoop my arms and release a murder to the wind.*

'Work' became the primal act of keeping my animal self alive. I was not an artist at the top of my game, like Matisse. I did not discover a new creative vision.

I was signed off sick / am still haunted by the shame.

Shame: the sticky residue of my internalised ableism. I wash it off, but it grows roots and they run deep. I wonder whether shame wound its poison tendrils around Matisse as he lay in his bed, too ill to attend the opening of his Chapel.

Today I exist in a liminal space: not quite bed-dweller, not quite out-of-bed either. I'm in a state of suspension, a long and protracted becoming

(what, I don't know)

Work is once more a possibility but I tread a precarious line: one project, one meeting, one Miserandino spoon away from a flare. My energy needs to be carefully conserved. I can no longer do things that I used to perform reliably and with ease. Like turning up at the office.

Just turning up at the office.

The getting up early, the getting dressed, the eating of breakfast, the rigours of the commute, the race against the clock to arrive at a certain time. These acts of exertion can send me reeling back to my mattress, depleted. Recovery takes days, sometimes weeks.

I work from home now, and my time off is mostly spent resting, recovering. Sometimes I work from bed, propped up awkwardly on pillows. My sanctum of sleep doubles up as a desk, a temporary office on days when I don't have the spoons to exist upright. My bed is still an anchor, the punctuation point between short bursts of activity, a prop, my biggest support. An aid that allows me to access work.

Living with a chronic illness has crystallised for me the physical investment that comes with holding down a regular job. We pay with our bodies. This is the invisible sacrifice we make: non-disabled folk, too, although people with chronic illness are disproportionately affected. Our sacrifice is higher, more keenly felt. I think of the photograph of Matisse, and the wooden cross looming over his shoulder. A shape which speaks of sacrifice, salvation, pain. I think of his body, laid out under it, labouring: an offering of sorts.

Today we worship at the altar of capitalism, we sing to the gods of productivity. Our bodies are our offerings. We are compelled, conditioned to drive ourselves to exhaustion, past depletion, to override the body's rhythms. Why?

Sometimes the reasons are economic: we need to work to afford to live. Sometimes it is driven by ingrained social expectations – there still exists a disturbing stigma around being 'out of work'. Sometimes it's the fear of asking for support: the contemporary welfare state and benefits system in the UK is an increasingly dangerous place for disabled people to be. Sometimes we are our own drivers: we need to work in some form to meet a deeply human need for purpose, achievement, and social connection – despite the harm it might do to our body-minds. Of course, it's not always a choice. Choice itself is a privilege.

The situation becomes even more complicated for those of us working in the arts. 'Work' becomes tangled up with ideas of a spiritual calling. An artist's gift is seen as something that transcends the grubby world of work. Matisse himself famously described art as a balm, a soothing reward for the good hardworking men (*of course*) of the world – 'something like a good armchair which provides relaxation from physical fatigue.' For him, art was a calling, a lifelong labour of love.

This idea of art as a spiritual calling becomes problematic when it is used to gild the belief that artists do not need to be paid for their work. As though they can survive on love, craft, and air. In these times of economic inequity, this idea is particularly dangerous for artists who are disabled or of other marginalised identities. A 2022 survey by Unlimited found that 87% of disabled artists had been asked to work for free. The majority of them had accepted, and often did so without getting their access needs met: one reason being that receiving payment causes complications with some types of disability benefits. The system conspires to keep the voices of disabled artists muted, firmly in their box.

I have no doubt that Matisse was oblivious to the role that being white, male, cisgender and already established played in the social mechanisms that allowed him to devote himself entirely to his art. Even as a disabled artist, he did not need to worry about being paid for his masterpiece: in fact he largely funded the project himself. Not all disabilities are created equal.

I know that I can't sustain the same punishing patterns of work that created the conditions for and worsened (even if it didn't directly cause) my ill health. But it's difficult to avoid in a culture that values 9 to 5 ism, presenteeism, that glorifies overwork, and that thrives off a manufactured sense of urgency. It's difficult to avoid if you're surrounded by managers and colleagues who are disciples to the grind, locked in a fierce battle to sustain their own position or climb to greater heights at any cost.

There is no easy way out.

So the questions that keep cropping up for me: how do we reduce the toll on bodies that already are working overtime to keep themselves alive? Is there a way of removing the body from the work?

I have been trying to do this. I choose and look only for work that I can do remotely – and from bed when needed, though I am not convinced this is a good thing. Our beds are sacred, personal spaces, and every time work encroaches on it, I feel I'm shifting towards a particular form of spiritual impoverishment.

I no longer attend meetings in person. I explain this to potential collaborators in my Access Rider: I prefer to communicate by email, as this takes the least amount of physical exertion. I can also take digital meetings, though occasionally I will need to take these from bed and may choose to keep my camera off.

(» Lazy AF)

The language is corporate, stripped of emotion. It's a sanitised version of my lived reality, made palatable for colleagues. There are things beyond the Access Rider that they will never see, that they don't need to know. I choose what and how much to disclose, and when.

Living with a dynamic disability, one that fluctuates day to day and week to week, is particularly difficult to explain, so I often avoid it. Many non-disabled people struggle with the fact that the body is an organic, changeable system that works to its own rules; or that chronic illness is endlessly chaotic, that it works in loops and whorls and plateaus and dips, predictable only in its unpredictableness. They need patterns, causes; they want neat narratives of recovery. A healing journey is fine as long as it happens steadily, incrementally, and by a certain deadline.

I failed at multiple phased returns to work: my body's attempts to heal refused to conform to a capitalist-imposed pattern of steady upward progress.

I am in an online meeting. I'm reduced to a face in a box on a screen: we are splayed out, neatly arranged. I turn up the filter function so my colleague can't see the marks and creases on my skin, my sickly pallor, the bags under my eyes. I am wearing pyjama bottoms, a TENS machine and hot water bottle strapped to my side, an electric fan and energy drink just within reach. All of these are out of shot. My professional mask reveals nothing of the sensations in my body.

Hold on, I say – my ear is bleeding.

I disappear from the screen and reappear, a scrap of tissue clamped to my ear. I tug at the fleshy part of my earlobe and it detaches itself. It comes off easily, like a perforation, soft–liquid sound as it tears. I place the bloodied chunk on the desk in front of my laptop and look at it. Tiny white slug. I remember how yesterday the skin of my entire face fell off and I swept the detritus into a jar for safekeeping.

I have no idea what my colleague is saying any more.

I smile, they smile back.

In an article in the *New Yorker* 'Art As Life: The Matisse we never knew' (2005), Peter Schjedahl quotes Matisse as saying 'That is what normal people never understand. They want to enjoy the artists' products – as one might enjoy cows' milk – but they can't put up with the inconvenience, the mud and the flies.' I think of Matisse's photograph. What messy bits are hidden from the camera's lens? What are the mud and flies of his disabled experience? Where are his silences?

The meeting continues.

My smiling colleague is well-meaning, sincere. Not chronically ill. We discuss future plans. 'I find it useful' they say 'to have an aim in mind, an idea, something to work towards. Can I ask you something?'

I nod, yes.

'What do you hope to be ten years from now?'

I am suddenly aware of the gap between us, the jarring disconnect between my disabled and their non-disabled experience.

I didn't know there was more than one possible answer.

'Alive,' I say.

Courgette Flowers

SUSANNA FASCIOLO

A cook, a housewife, a caregiver,
a cleaner, a nurse, a shopkeeper.

They came before me, raised me, supported me and populated my everyday life with their stories and their values. Then it was my turn to leave their home and be something. And I myself have been a cleaner, a cook, a waitress, a barmaid. Work is inescapable, absorbing and I have so much conflict within it.

For twenty years I spent my days chopping, pouring, burning, scrubbing, holding and serving. The effects of these actions on my body are tangible and persistent, even now that I have swapped trays, buckets and crates for spreadsheets and *kind regards*. Physical work will always be there. In 2020 I had long phone calls with four women in my family. We were all separated by lockdown restrictions and we indulged in the following reflections.

I talked on the phone with Marina during her afternoon break on a double shift day.

The second phone call was with Elena, often interrupted by her children or other family members that needed her attention.

The third phone call, with Bianca, opened a window onto the lack of support certain workers encounter.

The last conversation was with Rosa, who is looking forward to getting her voice heard.

Marina was at first afraid that she wouldn't know the answers to my questions.

On an average day she works in the morning, then goes home to rest for a few hours and goes back to work in the afternoon. While she was lying on the bed, with her feet up, we had our phone call.

She started to work when she was very young, around 11 years old, in her mother's shop. She is now 65 and as much as she is tired and ready to take some rest, she sees work as a means to be an active member of society. Her role in the community is defined by her work, if she wasn't working she would see herself as a burden for her family or as a marginalized person. Through working in the family business for 40 years she built and maintained a network of relationships, holding space for others to meet and be part of a community. Eventually they decided to sell the small family business and when she was 50, holding a high school diploma and needing to support her children, she had to start a new professional life.

The many jobs she has had since then include: cooking in and managing her own cafe, taking care of elders and children, cleaning houses, working in shops. She has now moved to northern Europe and works in a restaurant: she cleans the kitchen and the dining room, she helps with prepping the food and cleaning dishes and pots during opening hours. She has a zero hours contract, which often worries her, but still gives her more security compared to the many cash-in-hand jobs she had back home.

Having to provide a service to others is what she has done most of her life. The continuous interaction and human contact forced her to build relations that sometimes turned into lifelong friendships, but other times turned into moments of vulnerability and feeling underappreciated. Over the years she has had to face people's complaints and attacks, their frustration and their bad manners. Service jobs demand that the workers take in the negativity from one customer without overreacting, and then move on to the next without passing that on.

So where does that negativity go?

She is now looking forward to retirement, to have time to read and grow vegetables, without having to expose herself to constant and unfiltered human interactions. She wants to nurture herself and the relationships that really matter to her.

Elena talked to me while hovering over her children's homework, loading the dishwasher, checking why the family's dog was barking. Our phone call is just a few seconds in when she tells me she will have to call me back, her mother-in-law needs her.

In her early twenties she was a successful student at the Academy of Fine Art in Rome. She didn't finish her artistic studies and instead she trained to become a health and social care assistant and worked in this field, precariously, for a few years. She was then a stay-at-home mother for many years and now that she is almost 40 she works full-time as a caregiver in a day center for adults with disabilities. Staying at home was at first a choice, but when she was ready to get back to work she couldn't find a job in her field. Then her current job came up, with a long-term contract, paid holidays, sick leave and hours that would match family life.

After tax she earns about €7 per hour, which is enough when combined with her husband's income, but seems low considering the importance of what she does.

Her tasks could potentially involve arts and crafts workshops for her patients, but not all centers have enough resources for that kind of activity, so most of the time she takes care of people's personal hygiene. Her work is extremely corporeal, involving utilising her body in the care of other people's bodies. She lifts, cleans, gives relief, reassures. The job takes a toll on her posture, her knees, her hands that she scrubs several times a day. She often has to use her own body to contain and control excessive movements of others, to stop them from hurting themselves or others. Her light blue uniform speaks of a clinical environment, but her gestures and expressions show warmth and humanity. The most satisfying aspects of her work day are the human interactions with her patients, their progress and their appreciation.

When the shift ends she goes home, where the work continues.

When she was younger, in her family of origin, she often made herself available to help in the family business or in the care of her younger siblings. Now she has created her own family and these patterns are repeated, it's the norm.

When elders in the family need assistance she is the one they rely on. The hours she spends at home are filled with tasks and requests. She pours love and attention to detail into her domestic work, and yet the recognition is not always there.

She talks of an 'imposed availability'.

Bianca called me on a Saturday afternoon. She is free from her day job, but she is doing some admin for her passion project. She is a trained and certified social worker, but that's not what she does for a living.

As a teenager she had many odd jobs in hospitality and retail. While at university she worked as a nanny to support herself. During the week she now works in a primary school, assisting children with learning difficulties or disabilities in the classroom. In summertime, when the school is closed, she runs summer camps with a couple of friends.

She works in the public sector, but she is not hired directly by the state. A cooperative is used as the middleman to hire workers, the state pays the cooperative €20 per hour, and Bianca only earns €7. The children she works with can be violent, she gets hit and bitten. She has to be calm, firm, reassuring and encouraging all at once. She has to make them follow the teacher, she often adapts and re-adapts the class to the child's needs, she has to put aside the fact that her contract is highly disadvantageous and that housing in Rome is so expensive that every day her commute is rather long. When she is at work with the children she feels useful and content that her support helps them develop academically and emotionally. She accepted this job because for now it is all she could find that is related to her studies, and because at almost 30 she craves financial independence and wants to be able to start a life with her partner.

When I ask her if she has ever done something that was not actual work but felt as such she says 'dealing with people's emotions'. Friends and family often count on her to be a good listener and a source of support and advice.

Care of, and interaction with, other people seems to be her main occupation, and only a small part of it is recognised and paid.

Rosa and I spoke while Italy was on lockdown.

Growing up she always had very poor health, so she decided to study medicine to get a better understanding of her own situation. During her studies she decided to leave university and train to become a nurse, to be closer to patients. She has been a nurse since her late twenties and she is looking to retire in just a few months.

She tells me how work saved her, because family can trap you and restrict you and a world outside of the domestic walls is necessary. She is comfortable in her role as someone that cares for others, whether her children or her patients, because she sees that as an expression of herself, but she wants to have the choice and agency within that.

Rosa says that if caring for someone is imposed, then it becomes a form of servitude. She is also aware that there is a contradiction in her generation: she was born in the mid '50s and as a young adult she, like many others, lived through that moment of sexual liberation, class struggle and the acquisition of many women's rights and political awareness. And yet, she still struggled to find her voice and freedom within her family.

Towards the end of our conversations we spoke about her plans for her imminent retirement. What will she do once she's free from work? Her response surprises me and makes me think further: she looks forward to having the time to inform and educate herself about politics, she wants to really know what is happening and make her voice count, because so far she hasn't had the time for that.

I Want to Dream of Leeks

ROSALIND REYNOLDS-GREY

I want to dream of leeks, Annie remarks as we walk away from the market garden we have just volunteered at in St Werburgh's in Bristol. We go to the community cafe and talk about pockets of utopia in an increasingly dystopian world. A thick layer of dirt cakes the space between my nails and my flesh and I take pleasure in picking at it whilst we revel in the joy of planting leeks and weeding nettles. It is so cool, we think, to do such an act not for our own personal gain, garden or produce, but for a community and in turn for our spirits which had been enlivened by these small acts of commune and growth. Surely, these are necessary spaces where imagined futures can be different from the declining and rough status quo.

I want to dream of leeks. Annie and I lie on my bed looking at cottages on RightMove, imagining a world where a home with a garden and a symbolic sense of simplicity doesn't cost upward of £500,000 rendering it a possibility only for the financially fortunate few. We imagine we have a cottage where we live, or maybe even a cottage each with a little path running from our gardens. Where we know our neighbours, where we are neighbours, and pop in and drink tea in the garden and tend to the vegetables and there is no world around us with all its harsh demands. Perhaps at the root of all of this, is a desire to abstract away from the systems which twist and bend and crush us. We will never afford such a cottage in the economic system we live under but the act of imagining, dreaming up a fantasy way of living gives us hope that perhaps a different way of living is possible. The following week we will volunteer at the market garden and our dreams will begin to be sowed.

I want to dream of leeks. I go to a community meal with a friend which cost £4 for three courses, canteen style eating in a run down building filled with the atmosphere of a family. We eat red pepper and tomato soup, scampi with chips and salad and a plum tart slathered in canned whipped cream. A little girl squirts cream into her mouth in such a joyous act of childhood glee I find myself once again thrown into a state of yearning for simplicity and connection. At the end of the meal, we wash our plates in soapy water and play a game with the girl who has been dismissed whilst the older children play pool. The space is one which exists to be nothing more than what it is, a way to save some food from landfill, to feed a community cheaply in an increasingly expensive society, and to bring individuals together – to shake off some of those barricades that render us individual and to remind us that really, we are all united.

I want to dream of leeks. And in a way I am. I am idly daydreaming often because I am signed off work sick and I am recovering: physically, mentally, spiritually. I am working hard to dispel the feelings of guilt and shame that accompany my sick days. My sickness sounds self-inflicted and my recovery sounds self-aggrandising, but at the heart of things, I am trying to get well. And getting well looks like taking time and carving out space and learning about who I am. I go to the allotment and I think, yes this is me: I am a gardener.

I have thought this about embroidery too, and baking. I am thinking it could be found in the ukulele or in woodwork. I am out there, somewhere, and I am sure I am dreaming of leeks.

I want to dream of leeks. And yet I find myself on the National Lottery website frittering away the small amount of money that I have on a dream of winning thousands upon thousands of pounds. I disgust myself with my desire for wealth but it's not so much a desire for money as a desire for comfort. I feel content in my absence from work and I have a sense of being grounded in a way that I have never felt in my life, but in the background is the humming nag of money, money, money. I left my job and am on benefits and living in supported accommodation and am very lucky in many ways to have this space and time. Yet, the world is expensive and money is worrying and wouldn't it just be nice to take these days, weeks, months and not feel like a drain on society or to be shamefully looking over my shoulder when I buy oysters on a Saturday afternoon and laugh and live? Can't both these things exist at once: a need for dependence on the state and a desire to embrace living with reckless abandon?

I want to dream of leeks. I go back to the allotment and kneel in dirt, sift my fingers through the soil and gently tug at weeds. The beds of salad leaves become sparser as we lift wispy roots from earth to bucket. 'Life is short and full of weeds', Alex remarks. We laugh at a statement that's truth is simultaneously full of hope and despair. Whilst there, I receive a notification informing me that I have an upcoming appointment with the Department for Work and Pensions. The bleakness of such a demand dulls me momentarily, the cool grey of the benefits office and its oppressive monotony casts a cloud across my thoughts before I return my focus to the dirt and connection of the group and the sun warmly grazing my skin. After we leave, I text Annie and tell her that I think we should be able to conscientiously object to work.

I want to dream of leeks. I buy two scoops of ice cream, rich and vibrant pistachio and biscuity sweet speculoos, sit in the hazy August sun and talk about letting go. We are weighed down and held back by imagined expectations and judgements from others. I talk about the fact that when I left my job and gave up a place on a course to take time for my recovery, I felt exposed and raw. With nothing external to hold up and present to the world, I am left with nothing but myself. And this self is not something I have felt comfortable being or showing or offering just as it is for my entire life. We acknowledge that it is difficult feeling somehow stagnant whilst those around you are moving, building and shaping their lives in external and confronting ways. Comparison has the power to make you feel infinitely small. There in the park, I realise that despite this lack of stuff to show for myself, I am moving in the direction I want to go. There are internal shifts and changes which are opening me up to the possibility of life and the abundance it can offer regardless of all those things which we are told will make us worthy. Thick splodges of ice cream land on my legs as the sun blazes, slowly melting away at those preoccupying fears.

I want to dream of leeks. And sometimes I wonder if I am too much of a dreamer. The weather gets wetter and colder and by late September I find it hard to drag myself to the allotment early on a Friday morning. The volunteering dwindled, and with it one of the few remaining things that I could hold up to society and say 'look I have value, here is something I do, I am worthy'. Sometimes, I lie in bed all day. My room is a mess of scattered clothes and the lingering smell of stale cigarettes. I am hesitant to write about the cigarettes, fearful of the further strike against my name, demarcating me as someone who wills themselves unwell and will eventually further burden the state with my unwellness. My mother was a smoker who died a slow and painful death because of it – she did not deserve to die, she deserved the care she received, she had value, she had worth. I say this for myself as much as for anyone else. I light a cigarette, tomorrow I will quit, I say for the fourth time this week.

I want to dream of leeks. There are leeks on the kitchen table and I am going to make a risotto and think of spring. The dark blanket of winter has enveloped me and I struggle to look forward. At points I feel like I am slipping backwards, reaching into old patterns, dropping into darker places. I am reminded that a linear sense of time and ideals of "getting well" are unhelpfully imposed upon us, and do not necessarily sit true with the experience of ongoing illness. Recovery has been conceptually appropriated by a neoliberal agenda! I think of myself as an activist as I gently lean into another reclusive, cold and rainy day. There is not an endpoint at which I am recovered, and what does it mean to move backwards anyway? Is there such a way that I can move backwards, or is moving forward just not as slick and mechanic as I was led to believe it to be?

I want to dream of leeks. I think again about comparison and choose not to look at it as a vessel for the entrenchment of fear and resentment, both of self and other, but rather as a gateway for hope and transformation. It is March and the rain continues to pour. For today, I resist the temptation to attach my ever shifting inner world to the fluctuations of the weather. Besides, all this rain is essential for life. I compare my life today with the life I had a year ago, and the life I had for years before that. They are very different lives with me as the tattered thread that binds them all together. It's not that there isn't more I want from life, or that I don't have more to give. It's just that it takes time, and that's okay. I live with someone who called me a sloth, referencing the amount of time I sit around playing backgammon. Though my ego was momentarily bruised, I quickly laughed it off. I appreciate the capacity to act in a slovenly way, I wish we all had that space and time. I know we all need it. I am grateful for the life I have today, and I am grateful for the experiences I've had which have brought me to today. Would I dream of a dream of leeks if it had been any other way?

*

I want to dream of leeks. More time has passed, things have changed inside and outside. It is March again, a different year. The Labour party is in power and what felt like a relief at first now feels like betrayal. The last few weeks have brought with them a relentless onslaught of talk of cuts to disability and incapacity benefits and the degrading and dehumanising narratives that go with those conversations. I am scared to share my thoughts, scared to share this writing because I am one of the recipients of those benefits. I do not look disabled. I wonder if I am a scrounger or a liar, if I'm undeserving and unworthy. I wonder if I have the room and the privilege to dream whilst living in the material reality of Britain in 2025.

I'm no longer completely out of work, I work part-time in a lived experience role in a self-harm charity. These benefits I am on have saved my life and enabled me to take time and exist at a pace that is manageable for me. I don't feel like I should have to hide that fact, justify it or be ashamed of it. I don't want to be ashamed that I have lived experience of self-harm either, but I am, and so I tell people my job title cautiously, and sometimes not at all. I carried shame when I was out of work, and I carry shame now that I am in work. Perhaps I'll say I'm a support worker or that I work for a mental health charity, I'll edge towards self-harm if it feels safe, and only if I can really trust that I will be respected, I may share that my role comes from a place of lived experience of self-harming and all of the assumptions that come with that. I'll share that my reality is one in which my mental health fluctuates and changes, that I can dream of leeks and give back to my community in millions of ways, some of which I am employed to do but most of which have nothing to do with work.

For me, the biggest contribution I have made to my community over the past two years has been to leave my job, focus on rest and recovery and embed myself in communities of people doing the same. It is within these communities that I have been able to offer help and support the journeys of other recovering people in a form of reciprocal mutual aid. There are times when I can only do this to a limited extent. And when I am unable to do anything and find myself with very little to offer, I have people around me who will step in and hold me and my dreams of leeks. I have been held financially by the precarious safety net of the state, and it is only through having that small amount of material security that I have been able to connect with a community where I can be socially and emotionally held and nourished and can nurture in return. The seeds I sow today in our garden of dreams are seeds of respect, reciprocality and empathy. I invite everyone to join me there, I ask those with power to come and take a seat in the garden, to listen to the community around them and to really ask themselves what values they want to live by.

Contributor Biographies

Vida Adamczewski is from South East London. Vida received the 2022 UEA New Forms Award from the National Writing Centre for her play *AMPHIBIAN*. Her writing appears in *The London Magazine*, *Mslexia*, *Document Journal*, *Ambit*, and *Vittles*, amongst others. Vida's debut collection, *Amphibian & Other Bodies*, is published by Toothgrinder Press.

Hattie Atkins is a writer from Manchester living in Edinburgh. Her prose and poetry have appeared in literary magazines such as *Gutter*, and anthologised by The Common Breath and Forest Publishing. In 2023, she received a First Class master's degree in Creative Writing from Royal Holloway.

Maroula Blades is an Afro-British writer living in Berlin. She received 2nd place for her project, 'Stones in Symphony', at the German 2023 Amadeu Antonio Prize. In 2020, Chapeltown Books published her book *The World in an Eye*.

Cat Casey is a fiction MFA candidate at the University of New Hampshire. She currently serves as the Arts editor of *Barnstorm Literary Journal*. Her work can be found or is forthcoming in *The Good Life Review* and *So to Speak Literary Journal*, among others.

Laura Celeste is a poet from the West Midlands.
She completed her Creative Writing MA at the University
of Birmingham with a Distinction. Her heresy has been
published in *bath magg*, *Magma*, *The Interpreter's House*,
Blackbox Manifold, *Anthropocene* and by the Young Poets
Network, amongst other platforms.

Rebecca Coxon is a writer and documentary filmmaker
based in Leeds. She recently completed her MA in
Creative Writing at the University of Manchester.
Her memoir *Inconceivable* will be published by
HarperCollins in March 2026.

Laura Elliott is a poet, short story writer and library
worker living in South London. Her publications include
One Horse Galloping Through Stubble Field, *Right to Left*
(2021), *this is hunting* (Distance No Object, 2019), and
lemon, egg, bread (Test Centre, 2017).

Susanna Fasciolo was born in Italy and lives in South
East London. She is a worker, and sometimes an artist.
She has back pain and no generational wealth.

T. Laundy is an artist and new writer who prefers to
not go on about herself, but her brain scans come back
'unremarkable', much to everyone's relief. She currently
splits her time between referencing the Frankfurt School
in hopes someone talks to her about it, and being unable
to leave the house, much to everyone's relief.

Susan L. Lin is a Taiwanese American storyteller
who hails from southeast Texas and holds an MFA in

Writing from California College of the Arts. Her novella *Goodbye to the Ocean* won the 2022 Etchings Press novella prize, and her published short prose and poetry can be found at: susanllin.com.

Kirstie Millar is a writer and the founding editor of *Ache*. She has an MA in Creative Writing from UEA. Her poetry book *The Strange Egg* was published by the Emma Press and won the Michael Marks Award for Illustration in 2023.

Naomi Morris is a writer originally from Birmingham. Her first pamphlet *Earth Sign* won the Hollingworth Prize in 2018 and was published by Partus Press. Her second *Hyperlove* was published by Makina Books in 2021. She is currently a CHASE-funded PhD researcher at UEA.

Hatty Nestor is a critic and writer, published in *Frieze*, *The Times Literary Supplement*, *Granta*, *The White Review* and other publications. *Ethical Portraits* (2021) is published with Zero Books.

Keev (Boyle-Darby) Ó Baoill (they/he) is a trans, Irish poet and writer. Their work has been published by Channel, Powders Press, theremotebody and Ache. You can find him and his work on social media @keevobaoill.

Tomilola Olumide is a Nigerian artist and writer based in Nigeria and the United Kingdom. Her interdisciplinary practice documents subjects as memory and identity, primarily informed by her formative years in Lagos, Nigeria.

Tomilola received her MA in Contemporary Art Practice (CAP) at the Royal College of Art (RCA), London, where she was awarded the 2024/25 RCA Sir Frank Bowling Scholarship. Tomilola received her BA in Fine Art from the University of Southampton, Winchester School of Art, and was awarded the Soho Global Fellowship by Soho House and Creative Futures Collective.

Cecilia Reeve (b. 1996) is a London-based artist exploring the intersection between Painting and Animation. She recently completed her MA in Animation at the Royal College of Art (2023). Before this, she studied Illustration (BA) at the University of Brighton (2018) and her foundation at Falmouth University (2014). Cecilia has sold work to private collectors and institutions such as Soho House and has exhibited her paintings with galleries including the Delphian Gallery in London. Since 2020 Cecilia has made several collections for Partnership Editions. Her work has been featured in *Its Nice That*; *Harper's Bazaar*; *Elephant*; *Die Zeit*; and *The Financial Times*. Her animations have been shown globally at a variety of film festivals such as the Sundance Film Festival 2022, the London International Animation Festival and BitBang. She has also been included in screenings at institutions including the ICA (London) and the Tate Modern. In 2023 she won the ArtsThread Global Graduate Prize for her RCA graduate film 'Porous'. In 2025 she held her first solo exhibition 'What the Water Gave Them' at Twilight Contemporary in London.

Rosalind Reynolds-Grey is an editor of *Ache*. Her work has been published in *Lumpen* and *The Real Story*.

She lives in Bristol and is frequently thinking about mental health, feminism and class.

Steph Roberts is a freelance visual arts curator, writer and interpreter based in the south Wales valleys. Her interests include health and illness narratives, disability, and marginalised voices in art history. She works with museums, galleries, and online to bring these stories to life.

Carrie Sear is a research analyst and poet based in London. She began writing poetry about her disability a few years after her diagnosis of Hypermobility Spectrum Disorder (HSD) and is particularly interested in using social structures and authoritative voices in her work.

Elspeth Walker is a writer and visual artist based in London with an MA Writing from RCA. She creates interdisciplinary works intersecting sculpture, performance, photography, writing and drawing. Focusing on memory, psychogeography, alternative archives and class. Her zine *Threads of Us* was featured in 'It all Starts with a Thread' exhibition at Whitechapel Gallery 2023-24, where she was also runner up Young Writer in Residence 2022. She has been published in various journals such as *Culturala* and *SICK* Magazine.

About Ache

Ache is an intersectional feminist press publishing
writing and art on illness, health, bodies, and pain.
Since 2017 we have published a literary magazine,
books and art prints by women, transgender
and nonbinary people that explore the complexities
of living with illness and pain.

Instagram: @helloachemagazine
www.achemagazine.co.uk